BABY AND THE WOLF

SHIFTER RESCUE BOOK 1

VICTORIA SUE

Copyright © 2021 by Victoria Sue

Cover Design by Vicki Brostenianc, vickibrostenianc.com

Edited by Sandra, One Love Editing

Formatting by Stacy Sirkel

All rights reserved.

No part of this book may be reproduced in any form or by any electronic or mechanical means, including information storage and retrieval systems, without written permission from the author, except for the use of brief quotations in a book review.

CHAPTER ONE

RYKER WASN'T sure why he was nursing a beer when he had a million things and probably a million people—okay, so that might be a tad of an exaggeration—needing his attention back at the pack house. Maybe he just needed a minute. He groaned to himself. Maybe he needed to get laid. Something to sort out why he'd been in such a bad fucking mood all month. He'd even snapped at Chrissy yesterday, which had nearly caused her to take out his knuckles with the drill she was wielding to fasten their latest cabin together. They'd been getting a little tight on space up to yesterday when they rehomed five omegas and their pups. Seth and Jesse had been fantastic, but there was only so much they could do with their small area of cabins, and he hoped Zeke was having luck with the land he'd gone to look at. It was in Tennessee, which was fine, but what they really needed was the parcel next door.

Maybe that was it? The uncertainty? He didn't need a run. Backing onto the Blue Ridge Mountains, they were hardly lacking in space or opportunity, but something was rubbing him the wrong way. He felt weird. Maybe the smell of the place was too strong for his shifter nose. He nearly snorted. The thought that anything about his six-foot-four brick shithouse frame would be sensitive was laughable.

He heard the raucous laughter from the group of humans at the bar and lowered his head. *Don't get involved.* He'd noticed the smaller guy with them right away as he had trailed in after them, and his wolf hadn't caught his scent, which had made the animal curious. He was downright gorgeous, with floppy black hair that fell in waves and ridiculously bright blue eyes. They were definitely humans, though, as the others all smelled disgusting, especially the bigger guy, who had ignored the barman's request to smoke outside. He was probably the boyfriend of the smaller guy. As Ryker watched, he threw his arm around the smaller one, pulled him in close, and tossed Ryker a sneering glance that screamed, *"He's all mine, fuck off."*

Ryker tilted his head and gazed at him, knowing his alpha wolf was irked at the not too smart challenge, even for a human. The move the guy had made could never be confused with protection or affection. It screamed ownership, which was ironic that he should object seeing as how he knew wolves were jealous, possessive, dominant SOBs with their mates, and Ryker knew with half a chance he would be one of the worst. But this was just *odd.* Not that blue-eyes seemed exactly scared—more like *numb,* if that was the right word. He didn't seem to be objecting to where the bigger guy wanted to put his hands, or was it that he knew protest was futile? Ryker inhaled slowly, trying to smell any fear. Fear had a bitter smell that made his wolf want to sneeze to get rid of it usually, but he couldn't sense anything. He must be overreacting. Either that or the cloud of thick cigarette smoke was screwing with his sense of smell. The bigger man leaned over to pick up his beer just as the smaller guy locked eyes with Ryker. He met blue eyes for a moment, while the man stared at him almost assessingly. Ryker was definitely tempted, but the bigger man seemed to realize he didn't have all of blue-eyes's attention and dragged him into the group. Ryker frowned. He noticed the wince on the smaller man's face, but then he turned his back on Ryker quite deliberately.

His wolf didn't seem impressed, but then his animal had been acting a little odd since they'd come to this same bar a month ago. It had been nearly empty then, but his wolf had caught the scent of something he didn't like. Ryker was passing through. This biker bar wasn't even in his rescue area officially. He'd just been restless, and while he always needed to be careful, his wolf was riding him hard, and he didn't know why. He should go. He didn't like being this far away. They had omegas at the pack house who would get ripped to shreds if the shifters they were running from ever found them, and Ryker wouldn't risk anyone just because he had wanderlust.

But it didn't explain why his wolf was behaving oddly. Unless he was getting senile. His lips curved in amusement. He might be thirty-six in human years, but since he would live at least another eighty, he wasn't even close to middle-aged yet.

The smaller guy hadn't attempted to turn around, telegraphed nothing to say he needed help or was even uncomfortable, so Ryker let it go. He met the barman's eyes as he stood up and threw some cash on the table. The barman nodded, understanding Ryker wouldn't be coming back.

Outside, Ryker headed to the far end of the parking lot. He passed the rows of bikes he'd seen when he came in and knew they belonged to the humans at the bar. He'd parked out of the way in case he changed his mind and decided he did need a run, but to be honest, he just wanted to crash. He climbed into the truck and started the engine, fiddled with the radio to find something he liked, and drove to the entrance. He glanced in his rearview mirror at the bar and resolved not to return, then returned his gaze to the front.

"Fuck," he swore as the figure loomed up out of nowhere, and he slammed on the brakes reflexively. If he'd have picked up any more speed, he would have hit him. He yanked the truck into park, but before he could move, his driver's side door was pulled open. Ryker gaped at the smaller guy from the bar.

"Please. Please," he begged, and his eyes widened as a shout went up from over by the bar. "I-I…"

He wobbled on his feet, eyes going glassy. Ryker lunged, his wolf reflexes making him try to dive from the cab to get to the man before he hit the deck, but he wasn't quite fast enough. Shit. Had he hit him with the truck? Had he cracked his head? Ryker reached out to the pale, almost alabaster face and touched his cheek to slide his hand around and feel for an injury, but he never got that far. The second he touched him, Ryker's

VICTORIA SUE

heart faltered, almost stumbling over itself in shock, then picked up such a thunderous beat it sounded in his ears. His skin prickled. Nerve endings all seemed to fire at once, and his skin seemed too tight to contain his wolf. For a stunned moment, Ryker thought he would lose control of his shift, and that hadn't happened since he'd been a teenager. He took a breath when his lungs screamed their emptiness, and almost blindly, he stared at his hand where it still lay on the man's cheek. This couldn't be what he was imagining though. There was no way he could have such a connection with a human. Ryker had decided the mating instinct was just going to bypass him altogether. But as his wolf howled in his ear, Ryker almost closed his eyes in defeat. It was impossible. Wolf and human pairings happened, but they were always fraught with so many problems, Ryker didn't think they were worth it. Apart from the obvious danger that humans could find out about them, the culture shock was usually too much.

He should know. *I should fucking know.* No, it wasn't going to happen to him.

The man moaned and turned his head. Ryker looked back at the bar. He could hear raised voices and knew the man had been missed. He'd been scared. The man moaned again and tried to open his eyes and shivered. Ryker took in the trembling man. Getting involved in human trouble always spelled disaster, but he also knew he couldn't just leave him. His wolf wouldn't let him, even if the human side of Ryker was sorely tempted. He could just drive to the nearest ER, he supposed, knowing full well as soon as the thought was formed, it wouldn't be happening.

He grunted, reached under the man, and lifted him as he stood, the man's light weight—too light—not giving Ryker's powerful arms a second's trouble. The guy gave a startled "eep" as he opened his eyes, but Ryker didn't have time to explain as he heard shouting. He deposited the man on the passenger seat and closed his door, shoving the stick into drive and gunned the truck. He glanced in the side mirror and saw more people spilling from the bar, but he was fast enough and far away enough by the time he took a right in a couple of hundred yards, the humans would have no chance of catching him.

He looked over at the guy. "What's your name?"

4

BABY AND THE WOLF

Huge blue eyes focused on his. "Emmett."

Ryker blew out a frustrated breath, knowing damn well he couldn't go to the pack house now. He would need to head back into town.

"I'm Ryker. Did I hurt you?" he nearly growled out.

Emmett shook his head. "I have a condition," he whispered. "I pass out if I'm shocked, anxious, that sort of thing. It usually only lasts for a moment."

Ryker grunted, but sheer relief rushed through his body so quickly his hands trembled on the wheel. "Where can I drop you?" He ignored his wolf's deep growl of disgust. Now that he knew he hadn't run into Emmett, Ryker was calming down. He didn't know what that had been back there with his wolf, but it was probably just shock that he might have hit someone. Humans were fragile, after all. And he needed to get rid of this one as fast as he could.

"I—" Emmett looked through the windshield as if the dark night would throw up some suggestion. "I guess a bus stop, or a shelter?"

Ryker gazed at him in disbelief. "We're not going to find a shelter within at least thirty miles, and then one with a bed at this time of night would be impossible." And there was no way. Even dominant as he was, his wolf wouldn't let him leave Emmett somewhere unsafe. He didn't answer, but Ryker could almost taste the sudden tang of tears. "Something tells me you didn't plan this through, huh?"

Emmett shook his head and hunched in the corner.

"What about the sheriff? I know—"

Emmett reacted like he'd been shot. "Anywhere here," he said desperately. "Just drop me."

Ryker all but rolled his eyes. He had no intention of abandoning the guy on the side of the road. He was a hundred and twenty pounds soaking wet, if that, and April got damn cold at night. Thanks to his wolf, Ryker didn't feel it, but he knew humans did. He could feel his animal practically pacing in his head and groaned silently. "Look, I'm staying in a cabin about five miles west. Just for tonight." *Or I am now.* "You're welcome to stay tonight, then you can give some thought to where you want to get dropped tomorrow. I can take you to a friend's?"

5

Emmett shot him a tremulous smile and nodded. Ryker nearly shook his head. Emmett didn't know him from Adam. He could be a vicious predator, and the irony nearly made him laugh. All he knew was the guy in the bar had to be pretty scary for Emmett to want to get away this desperately. He pointed the truck toward the cabin. He didn't ask questions because he couldn't afford to care about the answers. Humans were trouble, he reminded himself.

It had been a couple of months since Ryker had been to this cabin. The pack kept them dotted around the surrounding areas for shifters needing temporary help without needing the pack house. It was always restocked after the last occupant, so he knew they would be okay tonight. In the morning, he'd give Emmett some cash if he didn't have any. He could even see if the human side of their operation could help him. He never involved himself with that side of things, but he knew Zeke kept some apartments for vulnerable humans who got themselves into difficulties or who were running from abusive spouses. They were generally given help for a short space of time to get on their feet. He could do that. He could make sure Emmett was safe. Ryker swallowed a growl. He would have to make sure he was safe, or the chance of getting his wolf to leave was zero to none.

But because he also couldn't seem to leave fucking well enough alone, he asked, "You're sick?"

Emmett seemed to hunch in on himself, and Ryker could have bitten his tongue. He'd turned off onto the track that eventually led to the cabin before Emmett answered.

"I'm not sick—it's just embarrassing. Kind of like fainting at the sight of needles, that sort of thing. It has a fancy name, but if I'm careful, we think I'll be okay."

We think? That didn't sound sure. And who the fuck was "we"?

Ingrained habit made Ryker drive the truck around the back out of sight and cut the engine. They sat for a moment, Ryker's wolf still very invested in the human. Ryker opened his door, which seemed to prod Emmett into action, and he scrambled out, following him inside. Ryker kept a keen eye on him, but he seemed to be staying upright, even if he shivered. Ryker wouldn't normally bother with the lamps as his sight in the dark was

BABY AND THE WOLF

just fine, but he knew Emmett's wouldn't be. He pulled the blinds closed as well. "Bathroom's through there. You'll find supplies, so help yourself. Hungry?"

He nearly smiled at Emmett's hopeful look. *Nearly*. He didn't want to get carried away and make the human think he enjoyed his company. Nothing so rash. In no time he'd opened a couple of cans of soup and gotten some partially baked bread from the freezer. He turned the oven on, knowing it wouldn't take long, and got out a couple of bottles of water. He could do coffee, but their options were black or with powdered milk, and he wasn't fond of either. Emmett came out of the bathroom just as he was ladling the soup into bowls, and he nodded to the table. Emmett slid into a chair, and Ryker put some soup in front of him. He returned a moment later with the bread. "No butter. Do you want coffee?"

Emmett looked up as if he were startled Ryker had spoken to him. "Thank you. This is wonderful, and no, I don't drink coffee."

Ryker watched as Emmett managed to put away a bowl and a half of soup and easily his body weight in bread to the point Ryker got up halfway through and put some more in the oven. He nodded in satisfaction, although why he should care what the human ate was beyond him. He inhaled unobtrusively again. He knew Emmett had washed up because he could smell the soap, but there was something else underlying that. He didn't know what, and his wolf seemed utterly fascinated. It wasn't a scent exactly. If he hadn't known better, Ryker would have said Emmett wasn't human, because human scent was usually pretty obvious. The weird feeling of connection he'd experienced in his truck he stubbornly dismissed as lust. He'd started out the night convinced he needed to get laid. Maybe that was it.

There was a small bedroom, and after they'd eaten, he showed Emmett where it was. "But that's your bed," he said in surprise.

Ryker shrugged. "I'm happy with the couch."

"But I can't take—" He cut off the words when he saw Ryker's face and just amended his protest to "Thank you." Ryker nodded, then turned to leave, and Emmett put out a hand to stop him.

His wolf reacted like he'd been shot, and Ryker jerked. Emmett

7

snatched his hand back as if it had burned. "Sorry," he choked out and nearly ran inside the room, pushing the door shut with a little too much force.

Ryker scowled. He should get his grumpy ass to the couch and forget all about the human.

Two hours later, Ryker opened his eyes at the warning his animal gave him. He lay completely still and watched the shadowed figure of Emmett creep about the room. For a human, he was actually quite stealthy, which surprised him. He narrowed his eyes as Emmett sighed, barely audibly, and came over to the couch. He doubted Emmett could see his eyes slitted open, and he kept his breaths slow and even. What the fuck was he doing? He'd bypassed Ryker's wallet, which was on the small table, and he seemed to be staring down at Ryker with a puzzled look on his face. Ryker kept still —almost unnaturally so—and much to Ryker's total shock, he felt the barest touch of lips on his. Emmett breathed heavily as if the exertion was affecting him. He straightened, and at that moment, Ryker realized he was fully dressed. Emmett sighed again and turned silently for the door. Before Ryker even took a moment to question his sanity, he'd shot up and clamped his hand around Emmett's arm and yanked him back around to face him.

He opened his mouth to ask exactly what the fuck Emmett was doing, but then the scent his wolf caught robbed him of breath. A delicious shiver of such glorious intensity raced over him in an erotic wave, and he was immediately hard. Emmett trembled, but Ryker didn't smell fear.

He smelled arousal.

Ryker pulled Emmett flush with his body instinctively and slowly lowered his lips.

CHAPTER TWO

EMMETT FROZE. For a second, the firm lips were moving on his. He knew it would be the sort of take-no-prisoners kiss that he'd always secretly dreamed of, but then as if Ryker realized what he was doing, he stilled. It took Emmett maybe five seconds too long to decide what he wanted and nearly threw himself at Ryker. Ryker grunted as Emmett clung on desperately and tried to get Ryker to kiss him.

"No. *No.*"

It was like being plunged into ice water. Emmett shook, this time not with nerves or arousal but with shame. His arms seemed to slide down from around Ryker's neck of their own accord. What had he been thinking? What in Emmett's reality made him think for one tiny second someone like Ryker would be interested in him? He stepped away but didn't get very far. Emmett dropped his gaze to where Ryker was still clutching his wrist as if he couldn't let go. "I'm sorry." Apologizing was good, right?

"Where were you going?"

Emmett looked up. He hadn't been expecting that question. To be honest, the almost kiss had kind of wiped that out. "I was going to leave."

Ryker nodded. "Why?"

"Because..." Emmett bit his lip and could have easily given way to tears.

"Because Barry will try and find me once it gets light, and I was hoping to be on a bus by then."

Ryker absorbed that. "Why didn't you want the cops involved?" Emmett closed his eyes. He could feel his heart start to pound, and he pulled at Ryker's arm. He needed to get off his feet. "Is there a good reason why you don't want the cops involved?"

His ears started buzzing, which was really a bad sign. He pulled ineffectually at the hand, but it was like concrete. Clouds seemed to fill his head, and then he was lifted off his feet and held tightly before being lowered to the couch. He took deep breaths, and when he was sure he wasn't going to pass out, he opened his eyes. He opened his mouth to apologize again, only to have Ryker's finger pressed gently over his lips. "No, that was my fault. You already explained the stress thing, and I stopped you from moving away." He lifted Emmett's hand, cradling it in his own bigger one while he examined it. "Did I hurt you?"

Emmett practically melted into the couch, but then remembered he'd been asked a question and shook his head. "You've been very kind, but the more I thought about trying to run in the morning, the more I thought it was a bad idea."

"And the cops?" Ryker pushed, looking like the question made him feel uncomfortable.

Emmett took a breath. "Barry's my uncle. Mom died when I was nine. He's my only relative."

"How old are you now?" Ryker bit out.

"Twenty." Emmett's face pinked. "I know I'm pathetic, but I have no money, and he's best buddies with one of the deputies. I've run twice, and the last time, Deputy Callaghan picked me up. He brought me right back to Barry." Emmett sighed. He might as well know everything. "I stole his car. I'm not allowed to drive because of the syncope, but I was only trying to get to the bus station. I would have left the car somewhere safe, and I took the back roads so I wouldn't put anyone at risk."

Shame licked at his cheeks. He'd been stupid—he'd never passed out unless he was standing up, and he didn't even have his permit, but that didn't matter. They'd threatened him with jail time or an ankle bracelet if it happened again. "I got a hefty fine, and I have to work for my uncle to pay it off. He keeps small apartments, short-term rentals, and I have to clean them." And most of them were disgusting. Plus the cooking and the cleaning he normally did, and it was never just for Barry. Nearly the whole crew hung around and he was expected to wait on them hand and foot.

"I saw you watching. I could tell they disgusted you, so I told Barry I needed to use the bathroom and took a huge gamble."

Ryker gazed right at him as if he was deciding if Emmett was telling the truth. "And the kiss?"

Emmett knew his face had flushed before, but this time it must have been scarlet. "I thought you were asleep. I didn't mean to wake you up. I just—"

But Emmett didn't get to finish the sentence because Ryker's lips fastened over his again. He moaned, melting into the glorious feeling of being trapped underneath Ryker's hard body. Almost absently, he wondered why he wasn't scared. Barry was a bully. Ryker was even bigger, but somehow he knew Ryker would never so much as lift an eyebrow in anger. He wanted this so badly and whined in reaction when Ryker lifted his head. He sounded gratifyingly out of breath. "I'm not going to take advantage. We'll leave early, and I will take you somewhere you will be safe. I know people. This isn't necessary and I'm sorry. I usually have more control."

Emmett smiled in giddy relief, but he almost didn't care. "I know. I believe you. This is for me. Please. I want this so badly. I understand you might not want me so much."

Ryker let his head fall forward, and then he raised it again. He tugged Emmett's hand to his groin. Emmett's eyes widened at his size, and for a moment, he panicked. "That's how much I want you," he said gruffly.

Emmett nodded and pressed his hot face into Ryker's neck. He smelled amazing. "Please."

Ryker hesitated. "This is important. You don't need to do this to get my help. That's unconditional."

Emmett nodded. "One question?"

Humor lit Ryker's face for perhaps the first time. "Only one?"

"Can we go in the bedroom?"

Ryker huffed out a laugh but stood and held out his hand. Emmett stood, and Ryker drew him in close. He brushed one of Emmett's curls off his face and breathed in.

"You smell amazing." He cupped Emmett's face in both hands and steadied him. "I have one thing as well. You can say no at any time. All you have to do is say no. It doesn't affect my help, and I am capable of stopping as soon as you say."

Emmett just reached up on tiptoes, aiming for his mouth. He still had to pull Ryker's head down though, and he exulted in the small, almost growl he heard in the back of Ryker's throat before their lips met. The thought of Emmett being responsible for that sort of reaction in Ryker set his heart thrumming. And then, for the second time, Emmett found himself lifted up. He wound his arms around Ryker and returned kiss for gorgeous kiss until Ryker managed to stumble into the bedroom, pull back the comforter, and lay him down like he was made of glass.

But Emmett wasn't. He was hard and aching and so desperately wanted to explore Ryker's body. Emmett wriggled out of his jeans while Ryker watched him with hungry eyes. It made Emmett feel about ten feet tall, and when he was naked, he reached up for Ryker before he even thought to be embarrassed. Ryker, who was still wearing his jeans, stretched out alongside him. He trailed his fingers from the dip in Emmett's throat all the way to the dip under his belly. His cock was hard and leaking. In Emmett's very narrow experience, he must be leaking a lot because he was wet underneath his balls. He felt almost sticky and for a second worried Ryker wouldn't think he was clean, but then Ryker dipped his head and kissed Emmett's belly. Emmett nearly came off the bed and reached for his cock in desperation. "Ryker." It was so damn good. Ryker's chest seemed to rumble in approval.

"Let's take the edge off if you're worried. We have time. I'll get you somewhere safe in the morning." He nuzzled the hair on Emmett's groin, and Emmett clutched Ryker's shoulders instead. The first touch of anyone's lips around his cock was indescribably good. Ryker was gentle but firm, and he clasped Emmett's hips firmly as he sucked. Emmett couldn't have kept still if his life depended on it, but Ryker didn't seem to mind his begging movements, the awkward thrusts his hips seemed to make of their own accord. Ryker hummed around Emmett's cock on his last thrust, then almost swallowed it down. The orgasm that hit Emmett like a train was the best moment of his life. If he died now, he would be happy. He groaned helplessly.

"Don't worry," Ryker soothed. Emmett suddenly realized to his shame he hadn't given condoms, protection, a moment's thought, and suddenly nerves kicked in. He remembered how big Ryker was. He bit his lip though. "We're just going to take things steady. You wouldn't be able to take me without a lot of prep, and I don't have any condoms with me anyway. I'm safe just to play. This is a one-off." He stripped his jeans off, and his cock sprung up, hard and heavy. Emmett's spaghetti-noodle limbs seemed incapable of movement, but he heard what sounded suspiciously like laughter as Ryker gently turned him over.

"I'm negative," Emmett whispered, regret and understanding filtering through. Not that he expected Ryker to take his word for it, and he wasn't about to say he was a virgin.

"So am I, but that's not just the point. I still won't hurt you."

Emmett closed his eyes and surrendered to the amazing feeling of being kissed and teased. By the time he was nearly delirious with arousal, Ryker trailed kisses from his throat to his belly, then went exploring with his fingers. Emmett moaned at the glorious sensation, and he desperately wanted to feel Ryker inside him.

Ryker paused as his fingers circled Emmett's hole, and Emmett could feel the slick on him. He might not have had condoms, but he must have had lube. It was so good. He loved the glide and tug, desperately wished it was something else, and started rocking his hips as Ryker inserted first one finger, then another.

He heard Ryker's breathing change and him mutter something about him prepping. "Yes," Emmett moaned, assuming it was a question. "Please. Please fuck me."

"I—"

"Please," Emmett cried and rocked his hips. He could feel Ryker just there and wanted it with everything in him. Nothing in his crazy, fucked-up life had ever felt so perfect. This was though. He knew it. He knew Ryker wouldn't hurt him, and he nearly cried in giddy relief when Ryker turned him on his belly and pushed a pillow under him . For a moment, Ryker held still, then lined himself up and pushed.

"You can stop me," he ground out. "If it hurts."

But Emmett simply pushed back, and Ryker slid inside. "Fuck," Ryker swore. "Emmett. Are—"

"I'm perfect," Emmett assured him. "Please move. Please."

As if Ryker was unable to help himself, he groaned and slid inside some more. Emmett couldn't speak. Could barely think. The fullness, the rightness, was utterly incredible.

"You're good?" Ryker asked again, an audible catch in his voice. Emmett pushed against him and gasped.

"So good." Which Ryker must have believed this time because he started to move. Cautious thrusts as if Ryker was scared to hurt him, but that drove Emmett mad with need, and he begged and cried for harder, for faster. Just at the moment where Emmett was going to tip over, Ryker pushed a hand under him and grabbed his aching cock, and that was it. Emmett came so hard and so fast, everything seemed to white out as pleasure so deep in his bones rushed through him. He finally heard the cry from Ryker's lips above him, and then he didn't much remember anything else.

IT WAS light when Emmett woke to the sound of the shower. Memory rushed in, and he smiled. He looked at the sun peeking under the blind and wondered why Ryker hadn't woken him when it was still dark. He didn't think for one second Ryker had made a mistake and slept in. He had a feeling Ryker never did anything by mistake. Emmett's heart started beating a little more firmly. What did that mean? If Ryker had deliberately let Emmett sleep in, it must be for a reason. It must be something other than taking him to the bus station.

Hope flared in Emmett. Did Ryker want him to stay?

BABY AND THE WOLF

He sat up quickly when the door opened and a gloriously naked Ryker walked in. Well, glorious except for the towel, which was a little disappointing. "I overslept." Emmett tried really hard not to cringe at the slight overstatement.

Ryker met his eyes. Emmett took in the stiff shoulders, the cool, clear brown eyes, and expressionless face, and his heart hit his boots. He could practically hear the thud. "I made some calls. I have friends who are involved in a charity providing new starts for...*people*," he added after a small pause. Emmett frowned, briefly diverted by the conviction he was going to say something else. Then he understood.

"You mean people just out of jail."

Ryker shook his head. "No, I don't. There may be some of that, but this is more geared at runaways. It's why I didn't wake you up. There's a lady named May who's on her way here." He looked at his phone, which was still on the nightstand. "You have time for a shower."

"You're not taking me?" Emmett asked softly. He could hope.

Ryker shook his head. "I have to get back." He grabbed his jeans and left the room. For a moment, Emmett didn't understand why. It wasn't like he hadn't seen everything he had last night. He swallowed around the tightness in his throat. Ryker had said it was a one-off. He'd been fair and direct with Emmett. Emmett scrubbed an irritated hand over his eyes. He'd been more than fair. He'd rescued him from Barry, and it looked like he was going to finally get a new life. He couldn't expect Ryker to suddenly want to change *his* whole life because of a one-night stand. Just because Emmett had fallen for Ryker didn't mean it was returned.

Emmett got out of bed and grabbed a shower. It was only when he washed himself and felt a slight twinge that he thought about what had happened. He wasn't completely innocent. To put it bluntly, his ass should hurt like hell, but it wasn't even really sore. Whatever lube Ryker had used must be amazing stuff. Then he thought back to last night. He'd been almost delirious with lust, but he remembered Ryker had held him still when he had come, almost as if he couldn't bear to move. As far as he was aware, Emmett had fallen asleep with Ryker still inside him, which was both embarrassing and wonderful at the same time. By the time he had finished getting dressed, he heard voices in the kitchen, so he plastered on a polite smile and glanced at the woman who stood in the kitchen.

For a second she blinked in seeming surprise, and Emmett faltered. Wasn't she expecting him? Ryker came out of the pantry holding some bread. "I was going to make some toast."

Emmett turned his polite smile on Ryker. He wasn't going to put either of them through this. "It's okay. I'm not hungry at the moment. I'm not really a breakfast person." He was starving, but he couldn't cope with being where he wasn't wanted. He thanked Ryker and turned, heading for the door. He was outside and walking to the Range Rover before May caught him up.

"Emmett?" May said gently.

He glanced at her. "Can we just go? I'm nervous my uncle will be looking for me."

She nodded and opened the car. They were driving away from the cabin a moment later. Emmett very firmly refused to look back.

CHAPTER THREE

SEVEN MISERABLE WEEKS LATER, Ryker got a summons he hadn't been expecting. Seven weeks where he was convinced every day he was going to lose his mind. Six weeks and six days too many since he had seen a certain human. Over a thousand hours too long to feel like half of him was missing. Zeke—Ryker's boss—had asked to see Ryker as soon as he could make it into his offices in downtown Asheville, which was as close to an order to get his ass there immediately as it could be. Zeke hadn't even called him; May had.

Chrissy looked at him warily as he put the phone down. "I've gotten called in to see the boss."

"Good," she mumbled around the nail between her lips, then took it out. "Go get your grumpy ass down there, and don't come back until you've had your personality upgraded."

Ryker scowled, but she just raised an eyebrow as if he was proving her point. He huffed and strode out to the truck, smiled at Louis as he passed because anything less would be like kicking a puppy, got the expected blush and lowered gaze, then headed to the parking area. He didn't really expect Louis to look him in the eye even after repeated assurances, because the last time he had done that to an alpha he'd had every finger broken, but he hoped one day.

He got into the truck and slammed the door, his heart pounding like he'd run a race. What the hell did Zeke want? Their friendship worked better when neither of their alpha personalities crossed paths that often, even if Zeke was a human. The corporate charity that handled the human side of the operation was a front for the shifter side of everything. But Zeke had his own reasons for what he did, and Ryker owed him. He'd even made him his partner on paper, but Ryker still thought of him as the boss. It had been Zeke who had put up all the money, bought the land, and ran the human side of everything.

Ryker did the hands-on shit. He was the guy who usually had to break into someone's house and rescue the omega or kids or mate that was being abused or treated like they were property.

Ryker mentally altered that. He didn't have a problem with ownership exactly, providing the person being owned was good with it and was treated right, but often omegas could get stuck with an asshole, and that's where he came in. It wouldn't be the first time he had stared down the wrong end of a gun barrel, and it wouldn't be the first time he'd been involved in a shifter fight to the death. He'd met Zeke because he'd done exactly that. Zeke had found him just after his so-called father had shot him after beating up his mom. His mom hadn't survived, and it was a wonder Ryker had because he'd been too weak to shift when Zeke had found him.

Not that as a human Zeke didn't have his own problems. He'd lost his shifter mate years ago. All the shifters involved with Shifter Rescue had been touched by similar stories, not that Zeke generally called him down to the office for that. Come to think of it, Zeke never called him down to the office, so he had no idea what was going on.

The sudden thought he might catch a glimpse of a certain human made his breath catch.

Maybe Ryker needed a change? Maybe that was why he was pining over a human. *Pining?* He felt physically sick. Like an addict desperately needing a fix. Maybe what he really needed to do was fess up to May and find out how Emmett was. He knew his wolf did. Dumb animal was barely

BABY AND THE WOLF

speaking to him. Not that it used words, obviously, but his alpha wolf generally had a way of making sure Ryker heard him just fine. He'd had a ridiculously awkward conversation with May a day after Emmett had left with her asking that if Emmett was at risk or anything to please call him. She hadn't, and it was killing him.

If May had thought that was odd, she had had the grace not to call him on it.

Another sense of unease rushed through him as he wondered if something was wrong. Ryker's heart started pounding. What if they'd done tests and Emmett really was sick? Ryker tightened his hands on the steering wheel. He should have called May again and made sure.

Two hours later, he was let into Zeke's cool offices. May greeted him with wariness, which settled like lead in his belly. He strode purposely toward Zeke's door, knocked briefly, and let himself in. Zeke looked up and nodded to the chair in front of the desk, but Ryker wasn't here for some interview, and he leaned back against the closed door and folded his arms. "Well?"

Zeke sighed. "Sit down."

Ryker was tempted to retort "make me," but he just stayed where he was instead. Zeke threw his pen down and eyed Ryker. He didn't know what was wrong with the usually cool, calm, collected guy, but something was riding his ass.

"I need help."

Ryker nearly gaped. That was a first. He sat and finally faced Zeke. Zeke was silent for a moment before he spoke. Just as Ryker was going to change his mind and stand, he met Ryker's eyes. "My mate left me just over twenty years ago, and I never found her."

Ryker nodded. He knew that. It was why they had met. "I know some panther clans make human and shifter mating pretty impossible." They weren't as bad now, but elitist didn't even begin to cover how they used to be, and Zeke was one hundred percent human. "Banned cross-shifter mating as well as banned human mating."

"They do. I obviously didn't know that. I didn't know shifters existed. Josie did, and that was the problem. She was a panther omega."

Ryker lifted an eyebrow in surprise. He hadn't known she was an omega. That was rare, very rare for panthers.

"Or at least he told me she couldn't shift and defend herself. I now know that's because she was an omega. And the Panthera found out about me. She went to visit her while I was away at a stupid work thing."

Ryker winced. The head of a panther clan was the alpha female or Panthera. Panther clans were very different from wolf packs. Members never lived together. It was even usual for mated pairs to live apart, and it was how Josie must have gotten away with hiding she had a human boyfriend.

"The Panthera frightened Josie into giving me up. She expected Josie to return to the fold. She didn't expect her to run."

Ryker sat back. He knew the Panthera would have threatened Zeke's life. Shit, that was god-awful. "But—" He cut the words off.

"Why did she go?" Zeke supplied. "Why didn't she talk to me first?"

Ryker arched an eyebrow, because *yes*.

"She was pregnant."

"Fuck," Ryker said. Wolves, alphas especially, could hear the heartbeat of an unborn child, but he knew panthers couldn't, or males certainly. The Panthera could, he thought, but that might have been just a legend. They were a secretive lot.

Zeke nodded. "Josie must have known, and she knew not only was I in danger, but a mixed cub would have been slaughtered immediately."

"How did you find out?"

"Because a week later I got a visit from the Panthera's son, Josie's brother. Her older brother. He told me everything."

Ryker gaped. That the Panthera could threaten her own daughter... "What did he say?"

"He told me all about shifters and demonstrated right in front of me. I thought I was going to have a heart attack. He told me basically that if I didn't stop looking for her, not only would I meet with an unfortunate accident, but so would she."

Ryker couldn't imagine. He hadn't known any of this. "And now?" Because there must be something, some reason Zeke was telling him. Zeke

BABY AND THE WOLF

was one of the most private people he knew. They'd known each other nineteen years, and this was the first time he'd heard any details.

"Emmett Keefer is my son."

For a moment there wasn't even enough oxygen in the room, but then Ryker took a breath and acknowledged in some weird karma-type shit way, he wasn't surprised. Then awareness slammed into him. *Fuck.* Emmett was Zeke's *son?* He gazed at Zeke, waiting for the bastard to leap up and go for his jugular.

"And he knows?"

Zeke shook his head. "I saw his file for the first time yesterday. I was out of state, as you know, when May settled him into a shared apartment. You know he has something that makes him react badly to stress? Vasovagal syncope to give it its proper title."

Ryker nodded, but it was unnecessary as his report contained the details of how they met, and Ryker had stressed to May he needed to be checked out by a doctor. "The blood enzymes we routinely run flagged him as a shifter, but not what type. I didn't know myself until I saw his picture." He pulled a wallet out of his back pocket and flipped it open. He slid out an old photo and passed it over. Ryker took it, and his fingers tightened involuntarily. Emmett was nearly her double, especially as this photo was obviously from years ago. So Zeke wasn't here to ream him out? But then he wouldn't know. May was a shifter, but after they had both showered, the only lingering scent could be explained by close proximity, so she couldn't have said anything.

"He didn't say anything to me. It was a total coincidence we met."

Zeke nodded, picked up his pen, and tapped it nervously, which was also a first. Fuck, it made Ryker glad he had no kids if they caused this much of a problem. "I know. I read your report."

"Why would Josie leave her son with such a bastard though?"

"I don't know. Josie told me she was an orphan. She'd been an only child, and her parents were killed in an accident. She was nineteen when we met and six months later ran off." Zeke looked at Ryker, the fear and the longing in his eyes warring for dominance. "He's afraid of his uncle, and I'm afraid of the Panthera finding out who he is."

No wonder his wolf had acted all weird in the bar. He'd recognized the presence of shifters but had not been able to identify them. He wondered if they were all panther shifters.

Zeke nodded. "I've done some more research since I found out about Emmett yesterday. Josie changed her name and must have been able to buy a whole fake identity. She died in an accident when Emmett was nine. Barry was made his guardian after she named him as her next of kin. Panther shifters always have the pack name as a last name, the same as some wolves, but because they are so independent, they may take a human last name. This was how Barry managed to keep Emmett's existence as a secret. The Panthera may not even know Josie is dead."

"It was reported as a wild animal attack while she was out hiking with friends. Friends who, after the accident investigation was completed, have since been impossible for me to track down."

So the panther clan had killed her. No wonder Zeke looked like shit. "Are you a hundred percent positive who he is?"

Zeke nodded. "Very. I know he carries no shifter scent. I already asked May. That's the one unique trait with panthers and the other reason I know what he is."

Ryker went hot, then cold all over. "What did you say?"

"That they carry no scent."

"No." Ryker shook his head. "You said omega, but that's impossible. There's no such thing as a panther omega born to mixed parents." Or as far as he knew.

It was Zeke's turn to shake his head, and Ryker's heart started pounding. For the first time in weeks, his wolf sat up and took notice. "That's a rumor put out by them to discourage mixed mating because omegas are so revered in panther clans. We know Emmett carries the shifter gene. He's a shifter who doesn't shift. He carries no scent. It's not impossible to believe that somewhere I have shifter blood in me. And likely why uncle dearest was keeping him in isolation. I'm not sure Barry hid him simply for Emmett's protection or why he didn't tell Emmett what he is. I'm still trying to find that out."

Ryker's heart pounded in his ears. His world seemed to be narrowing to a tight tunnel. He almost couldn't breathe. "Do panther omegas have the same gifts as wolf omegas?"

"Yes. In females it obviously doesn't matter, but in males it's a huge problem, as you can imagine."

"Spell it out," Ryker said gruffly just in case his whole fucking world hadn't turned on its head.

Zeke looked uncomfortable. "It's not like I've been able to run tests. May says he's a very private person and completely convinced if he shows any sign of his condition, he will be penalized somehow. You really think I'm going to sit him down and say, 'Oh, by the way, son, not only could your mother turn into a wild animal at will, but we have an awful feeling that you can get pregnant'?" Zeke's voice rose with each word. "He has no idea who his mom was or who he is."

"And what do you want me to do?" He had to talk to him. Somehow get him on his own after Zeke had broken the news.

"I'm afraid to tell him," Zeke admitted. "Stress—"

"I know," Ryker interrupted, and then understanding slammed into him. "Wait. You expect *me* to tell him?" *Fuck.*

"May tells me he asks about you. Not often, but he has inquired if he's ever likely to see you again. She told him you do a lot of traveling," he said dryly. "But seeing a friendly face might calm him down enough it's not such a shock."

Ryker scoffed disbelievingly. Nothing would make that news any better. Ryker closed his eyes and thought back. Not that he'd had to think very much. Their whole interaction had been running around his mind on repeat for weeks. He'd thought Emmett had prepped, but if Ryker hadn't been so lust addled, he would have known that was ridiculous. He was just on his way out, for fuck's sake. Omegas didn't need lube when they were in heat. And if he was in heat, it explained why Ryker's body had reacted as it did.

I knotted him. Ryker hadn't been able to pull out after he had come, and it was only because Emmett had practically passed out from exhaustion that he hadn't realized. He was so fucking stupid. He knew. His wolf had been trying to tell him at the time, and his normally ironclad control had disappeared like so much smoke.

It also meant something else. There might not be any point in warning Emmett about the insane possibility of a male getting pregnant anymore. In fact, it was probably already too late.

CHAPTER FOUR

EMMETT CLOSED his bedroom door and leaned against it in relief. He liked making friends, but Mark and Katy were both a little over the top. Katy had gone to class and Mark to his part-time job, so he had the apartment to himself. He knew he should be starting school as well, but he couldn't seem to summon any enthusiasm or any energy. May had done her best to encourage him to look through lots of options at first, but then she'd done a mysterious one-eighty and said there was no rush. He should be enthusiastic, grateful, and grabbing at his life with both hands, but when the doctor had advised he get his eating and routine sorted first, he had agreed with relief. He knew the doctor wasn't happy with him– he wanted to run more tests–but Emmett was reluctant and wasn't sure why.

No, he knew. If he was honest, he didn't want them to find anything else wrong. He was odd enough. He hadn't passed out at all since he'd gotten the apartment. Sure, he'd felt floaty a few times, but he'd treated each occasion as a warning signal and sat down quickly. It wasn't that. He felt like he was coming down with something, but he didn't know what, and he wasn't going to be labeled weak or even a hypochondriac. But he was scared. He knew there was something wrong. Something *else*, and he didn't know how long he could pretend there wasn't.

He knew he could be relocated. That was also an option. And he had briefly thought a new start might be exactly what he wanted. May thought he was scared of his uncle, and while the thought of seeing Barry didn't thrill him, the organization's lawyers had said his very small fine had been paid last year. Another thing his uncle had lied about. He also didn't have an official diagnosis as he'd never seen a doctor, so Barry had also lied when he said he couldn't get his permit. The only thing Barry hadn't lied about was the money his mom had left him. Twenty thousand dollars wouldn't buy a lot, but it was a nice cushion. Unfortunately, he couldn't access it at all until he was twenty-one. About four years after his mom died, he'd come across a letter that had gotten wedged behind one of the drawers he was cleaning, and it had been addressed to Barry Smith, but it was in reference to his mom. It confirmed that there was no way that the funds could be used—even for hardship—before Emmett was twenty-one. It suggested going to a lawyer. The letter had told Emmett two things though. First, his uncle had tried to get his hands on the money, and second, Emmett just had to wait it out until he was twenty-one. He didn't trust his uncle further than he could throw him, and he had no intention of asking him anything. Once he was twenty-one and free then he would find out on his own. The night he had met Ryker was just because he couldn't take it anymore. Barry hadn't let him out of his sight for months, and the closer he got to his birthday, the less he trusted him.

Now he had the opportunity to leave again, and he couldn't bring himself to. It was pathetic and needy and made no sense.

Ryker.

He was convinced if he moved, he would never see him again. He knew in his head that after so many weeks he wasn't going to anyway, but his heart wasn't on board with that plan.

He really needed to contact the names May had given him about getting a part-time job, but he didn't understand why she had been so reluctant recently. He was living here for free and even got an allowance toward food, which seemed incredibly generous and couldn't go on indefinitely, even though he doubted he had the strength to hold down a job down at the moment. He ought to get a job that included food though, because even though he was getting regular meals, he could happily eat what Katy and Mark had between them as well as his own portion. He'd always been odd about food. Always hungry but never put on weight, but then the junk his uncle gave him wasn't exactly full of protein.

A knock at the door briefly made him jump, but he knew no one could get into the building without a passkey and the lobby was covered with video surveillance. There were even panic buttons in the apartments, which had shocked Emmett, but apparently they had some adults who needed protection from abusive spouses, so he supposed it made sense. He still gazed through the peephole in the door though.

Then he did it again to make sure he wasn't hallucinating. He had the door open so fast after that it was a wonder it was still on its hinges. But then sometimes he surprised himself with his own strength.

"Ryker." He smiled and stepped back to let him in, his heart beating a little too fast. He headed for the small table and sat immediately before his body started getting any stupid ideas. When he realized Ryker had followed him but not said a word, he gazed at him carefully and his excitement fizzled out. Ryker looked like this was the very last place he wanted to be. "What's wrong?"

Ryker jerked his head up from gazing at the floor as if he was surprised at Emmett's bluntness. Emmett shrugged. "I doubt this is a social call." And suddenly he was furious at himself for being this pathetic. He would get rid of him, then call May and request a relocation. It was time to get on with his life. Fuck, it was time to actually *start* his life.

Ryker nodded as if he had spoken. "I have something to tell you, and it's going to take a while." Ryker focused on him. "You've seen the doc?"

"I'm sitting down. Don't worry."

Ryker blinked, but then his frown cleared a little. "I don't mean that. You've lost weight, and you didn't have any to lose."

And of course, Emmett's stomach chose that moment to growl. "I haven't had breakfast yet." Well, not if you didn't count cereal and toast. He knew he'd lost a little weight. Too much probably.

Ryker nodded again and pulled his phone out of his pocket. "Yeah, can you send two full breakfasts up to 528?"

VICTORIA SUE

Emmett's mouth fell open as Ryker put the phone down. "What are you doing?"

"Eating. I'm hungry," he said reasonably.

"But who were you talking to?"

"May. You know her."

"Of course I know her," Emmett said in exasperation. "But she's not some delivery guy. You just can't—"

"Sure I can. She offered. She was just waiting to see what we wanted."

Ryker was lying. Emmett wasn't sure how he knew, and he doubted he wanted to call him on it, so he changed tack. "You haven't said why you're here."

"I can't visit? *Fuck.*" Ryker scrubbed a hand over his eyes, and Emmett took pity on him. It seemed like this was hard for Ryker as well.

"Do you want coffee or some tea?" Emmett offered.

"I'll get it." Ryker headed for the kettle.

Emmett assumed they would get to the reason he was here eventually, so he needed to be patient. After all, the last thing he wanted was for Ryker to leave, despite his earlier bravado. Emmett gazed hungrily at his massive body, all six foot whatever of him. He could look his fill now that Ryker had his back turned. Massive thighs encased in washed denim tapering to a slim waist, then muscles spreading out along his massive back. Emmett could see them rippling under the plain black T-shirt he wore. Dark, almost military-short hair and a trimmed beard that had felt fabulous on his skin. And those arms. If Emmett closed his eyes, he could feel them around him. Warm, strong, protective. And so damn hot. His cock twitched in agreement. But then the memory of Ryker had fueled every erotic moment he'd had in the last seven weeks. He'd just thought he would always be a fantasy.

"Hey, Emmett, you okay?"

Emmett opened his eyes at the touch of Ryker's fingers. Ryker looked worried. Must have been because he had his eyes closed. He nodded and with reluctance moved his head back away from Ryker's touch before he did something rash. Like try and kiss him.

"I'm fine."

BABY AND THE WOLF

Ryker put down a mug of tea in front of him. It was peppermint, supposed to reduce anxiety, and Emmett found it a little funny that Ryker hadn't even asked, just assumed. Ryker glanced down at it. "You said you don't drink coffee."

That he remembered sent a silly pulse straight to Emmett's heart. It was ridiculous. *He* was ridiculous. He wrapped his hands around the warm mug and leaned forward. "You were going to explain why you're here." Because there would be another reason. A practical one. Not the one his silly heart was flip-flopping over.

Ryker nodded and pulled out the other chair. He took a sip of his coffee, then winced. "I don't know where to start."

Emmett could say all sorts of smart-ass things, but he didn't. "Then tell me why it's the first time you've come to see me." He wasn't sure he could physically handle being told it would be the last.

Ryker pinned him with his gorgeous brown eyes. If Emmett looked hard enough, he imagined he could see a gold glint in them. "The organization that operates these apartments, the charity, has another side to it."

He knew it wasn't the answer to his question. Emmett's eyes widened, but Ryker shook his head. "No, crap, that sounds like the fucking mafia. I don't mean that. Nothing like that. It's just the side you see only applies to humans."

"As opposed to animals?" Emmett guessed. That was cool.

Ryker winced. "Kind of."

"Why is a charity helping animals a problem?" Emmett asked, bewildered. He didn't get why that was so unusual. There were lots of animal charities.

"Because in this one, the animal and the human are the same thing."

"Huh?" Emmett wrinkled his nose.

"Look, there's no easy way to say this, but I can shift—as in my whole body can—into a wolf."

Emmett gaped.

"There's a whole group of different shifters. Bears, wolves, panthers. The tiger shifter is extinct in the US, but there—"

"Get out."

Ryker jerked. "I know it's—"

"I said *get out*." How could he? How could he come here with this fucking nonsense? Tears threatened.

"Emmett. I'm not—"

"Why?" he interrupted again. "Why do you have to come here with this utter shit? Don't you think it was hard enough walking away from you? Don't you have enough guys you can—" Emmett snapped his lips closed and stood up from the table. "I said get out."

"Sit back down."

Emmett shook his head.

"I said sit the fuck down. I'm about to prove it to you, and I don't want you keeling over." Ryker thundered the words, and Emmett was so stunned at his raised voice, he sat. It was actually a good idea to sit his shaky ass down anyway. At least he wasn't turned on anymore. Every cloud and all that.

Ryker stood up and grabbed the bottom of his shirt and pulled it over his head.

"What are you doing," Emmett squeaked out.

"I don't want my clothes tearing."

Emmett had no reply to that, just watched in astonishment as Ryker kicked off his boots and jeans. If he'd had any spit in his mouth, he would have swallowed. For a second, he even considered pressing the panic button. There was clearly something wrong with Ryker. He needed help.

"I won't hurt you." Emmett met his eyes again, and Ryker's face softened into a smile. "Just stay seated and don't worry. I promise, I won't hurt you."

Then, Ryker seemed to shimmer in front of him. Emmett rubbed his eyes. He closed his eyes, counted to five, then opened them again. Nope, a huge black wolf really was standing in his tiny kitchen.

Emmett took a few steady breaths. His instinct was to run, but his legs wouldn't have held him. Then the wolf shimmered, and Ryker stood in its place. Emmett looked down accusingly at his tea.

Ryker strode over and hunkered down in front of him. "You feel okay?"

"Peachy," Emmett whispered. His mind was going a million miles an hour. "That was real?" And he was naked. His brain was screaming it had just seen the impossible, while his body was definitely screaming something else

Ryker nodded solemnly. "It was why I was so secretive. The organization chiefly helps shifters who are in trouble and can't for obvious reasons get human help."

Emmett frowned. He couldn't believe—it was impossible—but unless he was hallucinating, Ryker had just changed into a wolf. He'd been so shocked, he hadn't been scared. "Do it again."

Ryker nodded and stepped back. In another moment, the same black wolf stood there. This time it sat on its haunches, then slid its front paws out on the floor and lay all the way down.

Emmett took a deep breath and stood up.

The wolf's ears immediately pricked up, and he rose back up. Emmett sat back down at the unspoken order. "Can you understand me?" The wolf nodded. "Okay," Emmett croaked out, and the wolf sat as well. Emmett reached out cautiously, and the wolf nudged his fingers. Did that mean he wanted to be touched? He wasn't a dog, but almost as if Emmett couldn't help himself, his fingers ran through the thick hair on his head. He dropped his hand, and in another moment, Ryker was standing there. He reached over for his jeans, and Emmett immediately regretted not looking properly. When he was dressed, he pulled out the chair again.

"I don't know what to say," Emmett murmured. No, he did. "Why now? Why couldn't you tell me weeks ago?"

"Because I help look after a lot of vulnerable shifters. If the human world ever found out about us, it would be a disaster."

Emmett nodded. That made sense. "I get that, but what I mean is why *now*. What's changed?"

"This is harder," Ryker admitted, and they both jumped as the doorbell rang. Ryker shot up and opened the door to May, who glanced at Emmett before Ryker took the sack and just about shut the door in her face.

"Is she one?"

Ryker nodded and put the sack down and went to the drawer. He found the forks and grabbed a couple of paper napkins. "She's a bear shifter."

"You're kidding me." May was tiny. Five foot nothing if you didn't count her hair and heels. Maybe she was a Koala?

Ryker smiled ruefully and pushed the food toward him. "Eat."

Because Emmett was still processing and hungry, he dragged the sack over. His belly rumbled again as he took in the number of containers, enough food to feed five people. He took a small portion, arguing that the amount was due to Ryker needing it. He guessed all that shifting took a few extra calories.

"Nope." Ryker shook his head and grabbed another one of the paper plates that had come with the food. He piled it high with amazing thick slices of ham, spooned a huge portion of eggs and potatoes on it, and then put it down in front of Emmett. "Eat."

Emmett blinked slowly. "But don't you need it? I mean, I'm guessing shifters need a lot of calories."

Ryker helped himself to a large plateful. "Yep, they do," he said quietly, then pinned Emmett's gaze. "Which is why I gave that to you."

It took Emmett a minute, and then he laughed. "I think I'd have noticed suddenly turning into a wolf." He looked down at the plate, and starving as usual, he picked up his fork. Ryker watched him until he seemed to think Emmett was going to eat it and then tucked into his own.

About halfway through, Ryker got them both some water, and Emmett chugged his gratefully. He eagerly ate the ham. It seemed expensive, and he always tried to fill up on cheap pasta. When he couldn't manage another bite, he laid down his fork. Ryker had finished his. Emmett had recovered a little by this time, and while Ryker had shown him something incredible, he still hadn't answered any questions.

"Apart from the obvious no-shifting thing, whatever makes you think I might be a wolf?"

Ryker shook his head. "You're a cat, a panther. You're never shifted because we think you're an omega, but you have all the other traits, or a lot of them."

Emmett absorbed that ridiculous notion but went with it anyway. "Such as?"

"I bet you're always hungry. You need a high-protein diet. I'm guessing part of the problem you had with passing out is connected. It wouldn't surprise me if you got a wrong diagnosis."

Emmett sighed. "I never got a proper diagnosis. Barry's friend has a sister who's a nurse. She wanted me to come in, but there was the no health insurance problem. She took a guess, and we went with that." He hadn't had as many episodes since he got here, and it was true he seemed hungry all the time, but he couldn't take any more than his fair share of what they all bought to eat. And lately he hadn't felt as well, even when he'd gotten the chance to eat more, which was why he'd worried he had something else wrong with him. Another thought occurred to him. "Why didn't you tell me before? I'm guessing you knew."

Ryker shook his head. "All shifters can tell other shifters by scent. Panthers are unique in that they don't have one."

Emmett frowned. "But that just tells you I'm not a wolf or a bear. Why wouldn't you assume I was just a human?"

Ryker dipped his head, acknowledging the point. "This is where it gets more complicated."

"More than humans turning into animals?" Emmett blurted out incredulously.

"I didn't know at the cabin you were a shifter. Everyone has standard blood tests run when they get here and that flagged you were a shifter. I was shown this thirty minutes ago." Ryker slid his hand into his jeans and took out a wallet and what looked to be a piece of paper. He held it out to Emmett, and Emmett took it suspiciously. He stared down at the picture and rubbed his chest at the sudden stab of recognition.

"Where did you get this?"

"My boss here knew your mom. He didn't know you were here or that you even existed until yesterday."

"Existed?" That was an odd expression. He stared at Ryker. What was he saying? "Why has your boss kept a picture of my mom all these years?"

"Because, I understand, he loved her very much."

VICTORIA SUE

Emmett managed to swallow down the hurt that was clogging his throat. "Why didn't anyone tell me?"

"The tests would flag you as a shifter but not what kind. As you have no scent, May was suspicious, but she decided to wait until he returned from his trip to ask."

And Emmett knew. "And he gave you this?" Ryker nodded. Even though he had to ask, he knew. "What's his name?"

"Zeke Coleman." Emmett waited, held Ryker's gaze until he shook his head. "No, he's not a panther shifter."

Emmett's stomach churned sickly, and he pressed his hand to it. *Mom.* That had to mean his mom was and she'd never told him.

"Emmett—"

"I'd like you to leave now." He stood up, ignoring his jelly legs.

"Emmett, please."

"Please what?" Emmett asked carefully. "It's why you're here, isn't it? He just wanted you to deliver the bad news. You didn't want to come here at all. Well—" He waved in the direction of the door and swayed. "—let yourself out."

In another moment, the arms that, up to a few seconds ago he would have given anything to feel, wrapped him up and lifted him gently. Ryker settled himself on the couch and kept ahold of Emmett while the room steadied.

"I've regretted every second since I let you walk out of my life."

"You didn't trust me," Emmett said bitterly.

"I didn't *know* you," Ryker shot back. He swallowed. "I want to get to know you."

Emmett ignored the tears that threatened to fall. "How do I know you're telling the truth? How do I know you're not just after some fancy job thanks to the boss's son?"

Ryker tucked Emmett against his chest, and Emmett closed his eyes with the perfection of it. He inhaled the delicious scent that seemed so uniquely Ryker's and didn't want to move, ever.

"Technically, your father and I are partners. He handles the human side of everything, and I run the rescues, the pack house. I call him the boss because he handles all the admin, raises the money. I'm a grunt, really."

Emmett let out a contented sigh. His heart beat steadily, and he felt stronger, which was a little odd. "The cabin?" He was curious, and while Ryker seemed to want to hold him, Emmett wasn't giving him any reason to let go.

"No. We have about forty cabins over a five-hundred-mile area. The pack house is like a secure compound near the Cherokee National Forest. It's where the most vulnerable shifters live." Emmett thought about that. "Your dad very much wants to meet you."

Emmett scoffed. "Why now?"

"Because he didn't know your mom was pregnant. He hoped one day he might see her again, and he built this whole organization because of it."

"She ran from him?" Emmett squeezed his eyes closed, but a tear still managed to escape.

"No, sweetheart, not him," Ryker said gently. "But it's not my story to tell."

Emmett considered that. "Will you be there?"

He felt Ryker's arms tighten and reveled in it. Ryker nodded, seemingly unable to speak. "For as long as you need me."

Emmett could only wish that were true.

CHAPTER FIVE

RYKER HELD EMMETT CLOSE, unwilling and unable to let go, and knowing full well he hadn't told him the worst. He could hear Emmett's pulse fluttering like a baby bird, but overlaid by a strong, steady beat that calmed his own racing heart. Strong meant healthy, right? Strong meant —*fuck*. There were *two*. Two heartbeats. He still couldn't scent Emmett, but his alpha hearing worked just fine, especially in such a close, quiet environment. If he wasn't holding him, he wouldn't have been able to hear it.

Now what?

A surge of such wonder would have knocked him off his feet had he been on them. Possession, rightness, clicked into place in Ryker's mind. Did he say anything? What should he say? What if it was too much to cope with? What if it was one shock too many? But then, how could he let Emmett out of his sight now? What if he did something that might harm the pup because he didn't know he was pregnant?

What if he hates me?

The second ring of the doorbell interrupted them again, and Ryker groaned. Emmett—who seemed to be happy being held—moved away, much to Ryker's dislike. He walked to the door, Ryker hot on his heels, looked through the peephole, took a deep breath, and opened the door.

Ryker's heart sank as he stared at Zeke. Couldn't he have given him some more time?

Emmett stared at his father for a few seconds before stepping back so he could come in. Zeke walked in, his face a picture of anxiety. Ryker didn't much care. "Sit," he ordered Emmett, but kept his tone as gentle as he could. "I'll make tea." Which meant no one could ask him to leave. Not that he was going anywhere. Zeke wouldn't be able to hear the pup, so he had a while to decide what he was going to do. He didn't meet Zeke's surprised look. He knew the man expected him to hightail it out of there.

Zeke turned his attention to Emmett. Emmett didn't start talking though, and satisfaction shot through Ryker. Good—he was going to make Zeke work for it.

"I'm sure if Ryker has told you who I am, you have lots of questions," Zeke said lamely.

"Why don't you start at the beginning?" Ryker could hear the way Emmett was trying to keep himself together and swore silently. How fucking long did it take a kettle to boil? He should be sitting with Emmett. What he wanted was to have him on his lap while Zeke explained. Shocks weren't good for him or the pup. He threw together three teas and brought them to the table. Zeke hadn't even started explaining. Ryker pulled out the chair closest to Emmett and sat so their legs were brushing.

Zeke gave him another surprised look, but he didn't comment on it. "I met your mom when she was nineteen. She told me she was an orphan." He rubbed his short beard. "You know what she was?"

Emmett nodded.

"I don't know what Ryker has had the chance to tell you, but panther packs or clans are different from a lot of other shifter groups. Not even mated pairs live together. They don't have pack houses like wolves or even large families like bears. They're very solitary animals, but they are very narrow-minded as well. The one thing they will not allow is mixed matings. Human and panther especially. If the clan had found out about you, you would have been killed. Josie never told me about her family because she knew the clan banned mating with humans, and she ultimately left me to protect you." His face softened. "She loved you very much."

"Josie?" He nodded, and Emmett once more fingered the photograph he still clutched. "Mom's name was Hannah Keefer."

"It would have been the identity she took as a safety precaution. She told me her name was Josephine Ellis."

"They would have killed her?" Emmett asked in a small voice. Ryker snaked a hand under the table and laid it on Emmett's knee. Emmett dropped his arm and covered it with his own. Ryker held back the smile. It had been automatic, and the fact that Emmett had sought him out for comfort filled Ryker with pride. He didn't think Zeke had noticed, but he was happy to go head-to-head if necessary.

Zeke nodded. "It was a mess. I didn't know that shifters even existed. I was just working up the courage to ask her to marry me when I had to go away on a corporate trip for my grandfather, and she was so *young*." He laughed. "I guess we both were. When I got back, she was gone. The apartment was empty of a few changes of clothes and her wallet. She left most of her things."

Emmett swallowed and looked down.

"Her brother, who I didn't even know existed, came to see me after a few days because I was making so much noise, as he put it, he was frightened the clan would come after me. I talked to the cops every day. Put up flyers. Canvassed every organization I could think of. I knew she loved me, and I was convinced whatever was wrong we could face together. He told me to stop involving the human world, as he called it, because it could risk her life. He also threatened me, not that I cared. Six months later, I started Shifter Rescue with the money my grandad left me, plus I had already diverted some of the business's assets into a charity. I always hoped I would find your mom. I never expected to find you."

Emmett looked like he'd been sucker punched. Slowly, he reached out a hand, and Zeke clasped it.

"Male panther omegas are very rare, that much I do know. May told me what your tests revealed when I got back from my trip. She didn't know you were my son." Zeke glanced at Ryker and seemed to notice how close they were sitting. "I asked Ryker to tell you because we've never met."

VICTORIA SUE

Emmett nodded. It was like he didn't know what to say. "How do you know I'm an omega?"

"There is a gene in your blood that's undetectable unless you know what you're looking for. There is a fail-safe on the computers at the labs here to identify it. When the computer flags it, May is notified. The only type of panther shifter that doesn't shift is an omega. It's possible you didn't inherit the gene, as from a mixed mating you have a fifty-fifty chance, but if that was the case, the computer wouldn't have flagged you."

Emmett nodded again, and Zeke leaned forward. "I never stopped looking for your mom. I can't believe you were both so close all this time, and I'd very much like to get to spend some time with you."

"It's a lot to take in," Emmett said quietly.

"And we need to do scans to confirm things," Zeke added gently. Ryker's heart thumped.

"What things?" Emmett asked. "You said you knew from a blood test."

Zeke shot Ryker a look. Ryker tried not to squirm. "I just want to know you're healthy. You need a special diet." The sudden tightness in Ryker's chest eased. Zeke had just chickened out as well. He probably thought Emmett had been through enough for one day. "It's likely you've been protein starved for a lot of years."

"Why don't you think Mom ever told me? She couldn't have known I was an omega."

"I'm still trying to do some research, but I have to be careful."

"Male panthers aren't in danger of shifting until they are teenagers," Ryker put in. "She probably thought she had plenty of time, plus it's not just *bam* and you have four legs and fur." He smiled ruefully. "I felt like I had the flu for a whole week."

"I'd very much like you to come and stay with me," Zeke said hopefully. "I have a penthouse—"

Before Ryker got the chance to nix the idea, Emmett interrupted. "Can you give me some time to process everything first?" He smiled. "I want to get to know you, but I'd really like to take it slowly."

Zeke nodded eagerly and sat back, releasing Emmett's hand. "Whatever you want. Do you want your own apartment? You share with humans at the moment."

"Let me think," Emmett said. "I just need some time to process everything."

"Okay," Zeke said and reluctantly got to his feet. So did Emmett, and they shared a brief hug. Zeke looked like Emmett hung the moon. Ryker knew how he felt.

"It's just so much to take in," Emmett murmured.

"I know," Zeke replied. He looked at Ryker, expecting him to get up as well, but Ryker stayed where he was. Zeke gazed at him for a moment. "Call and see me before you go. I have a new area I need you to look at. It's large enough for a full pack house, and it looks like you're getting the acres you need next door as well."

Ryker nodded once. He didn't know what their exact plans were with the extra land, but more space was always a good thing. It was clear Zeke wanted to ask about Emmett, but he didn't know what to say. He stayed sitting when Emmett got back from showing Zeke out. Emmett glanced at the clock. "Katy will be back from class in a moment."

But Ryker wanted to spend more time with Emmett. A lot more time, and he especially didn't want him out of his sight. "Would you like to see the pack house?"

Emmett looked at him in surprise, and then genuine pleasure shone from him. "I'd love to, but am I allowed?"

Ryker nodded firmly. "You're Zeke's son—of course you're allowed. Plus, you're a shifter." He didn't say what else Emmett was. "And I thought you might like to get out of here."

Emmett nodded eagerly.

"Go get a change of clothes in case we decide to stay tonight, then. It's nearly two hours with traffic each way. I'll call Zeke."

Emmett went to pack. Ryker didn't call Zeke, but he texted him to say Emmett wanted to see the pack house and Ryker thought it was a good idea to try and introduce him to what they did. Zeke's reply was enthusiastic. Ryker promised to let him know when he brought Emmett back.

Ryker escorted Emmett to the truck. Emmett seemed happy to allow

Ryker's hand on his back, sometimes a steady arm on his as they went down a few steps, opening the door for him.

"I won't break, you know."

Ryker chuckled. So much for him thinking he'd gotten away with it. "I know."

"But?" Emmett said, a small smile finally teasing at his lips.

"Humor me."

Ryker started and failed to tell Emmett about omegas a million times on the way to the pack house. Ryker's wolf was desperately wanting to come out and meet Emmett properly as well. Not that Ryker blamed him. He'd teased the poor animal by changing twice without so much as a run. No, he'd get him home and— Ryker's thoughts just about screeched to a halt.

Home?

A million times, *yes*. He shouldn't have ignored his wolf when it tried to tell him when they met. But then what if it wasn't what Emmett wanted? Could Ryker live in an apartment? Thousands of shifters did, but he could hardly commute nearly four hours a day. He had responsibilities to the pack house. And Emmett was so young. *Fuck*, he was going to make a mess of the whole thing.

"Tell me about you."

Ryker shot a look at Emmett. His mate was gorgeous. A pale pink flush stained his cheeks, and his eyes sparkled with excitement. "I can't believe with everything that's been thrown at you this morning you're not..."

"Hiding under a bed? Locked in a closet?" Emmett teased. "I'll be honest, I'm still not convinced that I'm not going to wake up and find out this was all a dream, but I want to be part of a family. I had it good for a few years, and I want that back."

Ryker chewed on that a moment. It sounded hopeful, but there was a huge difference between wanting to be part of a family and having your own kids. Especially with someone sixteen years your senior. Shifters never cared about that sort of thing. Your mate was your mate, end of story. Which was why Ryker had always avoided humans before. Emmett wasn't a human, but he'd been brought up as one, and you couldn't suddenly do a one-eighty on your beliefs in a single morning.

"I'm glad." Ryker didn't realize he'd blurted that out until Emmett looked at him.

"Glad I want to be part of a family?"

Ryker reached over the console and grabbed Emmett's hand. Emmett's lips parted as if he was going to say something. "Yes, but I'm glad you're a shifter."

"But I don't shift." Emmett said it like he was trying to puzzle out something.

"Doesn't matter," Ryker said. "You're still a shifter."

Emmett smiled shyly but, more importantly, didn't take back his hand. They were silent for a while, but then Ryker took a breath and started talking.

"There was me, Mom, and my father, who was the alpha of a pack back in Oregon. He was a lazy alpha, especially when he started drinking, and a crap husband all the time. Anyway, shifters were becoming even rarer, and we were struggling to keep the pack operational. Another pack—a much larger one—wanted our land, and he was challenged. It should have been a traditional challenge."

"What's one of those?"

"A fight. It can be to the death, or they can agree to just submit to the winner, but Dad thought he could negotiate. Thought he could let the other alpha run things and still keep his perks. Stay in the pack house and let the gammas do the hunting for him. The other alpha took over and gave us a cabin on the outskirts of the pack. He didn't have to even give us that, but he did. Things went downhill rapidly after that. Ninety-five percent of what we ate I caught because he spent all of our money on booze. He was always a bully, but he was ten times worse when he'd been drinking, and when he was drinking, he blamed everything on my mom." If Ryker hadn't been driving, he would have closed his eyes. He could still smell the blood. He'd always wondered when he was little why he never got a naming ceremony, the traditional way of welcoming new shifters to the pack, until he found out why he wasn't something his father was proud enough of to even name. So as an adult, he'd taken his mom's name and become Ryker Sullivan.

VICTORIA SUE

"Mom had to get a job. She made friends with the new alpha's mate, and my father didn't like that. Our old, beat-up truck died on her one day while she was coming home, and one of the betas gave her a ride."

Ryker swallowed. He'd only told this story to Zeke and Chrissy. Twice in nearly twenty years. He felt Emmett's fingers tighten in his, and his wolf calmed.

"I arrived five minutes too late. He'd sent me on some stupid errand to buy booze for him from a guy that didn't ask questions about how old I was. I came back and could hear Dad arguing with his former beta, and the guy was furious. He'd said all Dad had to do was keep quiet, and they'd have it made. I walked in, and Mom was lying dead on the floor, blood everywhere. The beta cornered me and told me succinctly that I had to keep my mouth shut or everything would be ruined. That they were onto a good thing and that we would be able to start our own pack with the money they could make with the scheme he was running. But I didn't listen. All I could see was my mom on the floor and Dad covered in blood where he'd beaten her. Dad was a big guy and a violent drunk, and he had a gun. He told me in no uncertain terms either I was his son and he'd make me alpha one day despite my mixed blood, or I was dead. I told him to go to hell, and he shot me before I even realized what had happened."

"Oh, Ryker," Emmett said, his voice shaking.

"Shifters don't bother much with guns. Maybe gammas if they're on guard, but it's very rare. I mean, what are we going to do with one when we shift? Too dangerous to just leave lying around. Anyway, Zeke was passing through. He was looking for your mom and scoping out the local area when he heard the shot."

"How old were you?"

"Sixteen. Believe it or not, your dad's seven years older than me." Ryker didn't believe it himself. Zeke easily looked ten years younger than he did.

"I would have been okay if Dad's beta had let me shift, but he didn't. He knew Dad was unreliable, and I certainly would talk. He took Dad's gun and put two more in me and emptied the chamber into Dad." He signaled and turned into a gas station, and they sat for a moment, Ryker's head full of the shots and the blood. His mom's body. Killed when he wasn't there. "The beta heard your dad's truck. I was bleeding out anyway, too weak to shift, and I guess he'd run out of bullets. If your dad hadn't come along, I'd be dead."

"I'm so sorry." Emmett squeezed his fingers again.

Ryker blew out a breath. He hadn't meant to dump all that on Emmett and mentally switched gears. He nodded toward the station. "Thought you might need something. Can you get me a can of Coke while I get gas?" He handed over a couple of twenties. "Get some snacks. I'm kind of hungry. Maybe see if they have a couple of bananas."

If Emmett had been surprised at the swift change of subject, he didn't show it, just took the cash and went inside. Ryker knew there would always be food ready at the pack house, but whatever calories he could get into Emmett was good. Emmett dutifully came out with a hoard of fruit and some chips, a couple of bottles of water, and Ryker's Coke. Ryker went inside to use the restroom and spied some protein bars on the way out. Maybe Emmett might like one of those.

Emmett was peeling a banana when Ryker got back, and he grabbed an apple. He threw the protein bars into the bag with the rest of the things.

"Do we have to hunt our own food or something when we get there?"

Ryker grinned at Emmett's teasing. "I thought you might be hungry."

Emmett huffed. "I'm going to be the size of a whale if you keep feeding me like this." For a moment, Ryker imagined the sight of Emmett naked. A taut, swollen belly that Ryker lovingly kissed. His wolf whined in impatience. *You and me both*, Ryker thought to himself.

"How many shifters live there?"

Ryker let out a relieved breath, more on solid ground. "We can take twenty in the pack house. Two to a room. There are another dozen cabins in the main area."

"And they live there permanently?"

"Not usually. We don't have the room. We have people who work there who stay on site, but the whole point is helping shifters get over whatever the problem is and relocate." He paused. "There are six or seven omegas there semi-permanently. They're too much at risk either from their old pack or mates to go back. We just had a large group leave, so we're pretty empty, but it doesn't usually stay that way for long."

"You're doing such a good thing," Emmett said quietly.

Warmth spread through Ryker at the praise. "I think we had a couple of new arrivals this morning, and there are more coming tomorrow. A local pack's been taken over. I wasn't there. Chrissy handled everything."

"Chrissy?"

Ryker glanced over at Emmett. There had been an odd catch in his voice. "Yeah, one of the betas. She's a mechanic. Her mate, Dinah, is the best cook you're ever likely to meet."

Emmett beamed, and Ryker pulled onto the track that led to the pack house. "There are five of us on the rescue team, but only two of us live in the compound full-time. There are a few from the ranger service who help, and we have a mated pair that does the housekeeping, that sort of thing. We have three gammas to provide security, but we really need more. At the moment we take wolves from other packs. They help us and we help them if they need us." The truck lurched a little, but Ryker wasn't worried. The roads were hard, they were supposed to be to discourage curious humans, because some people took no notice of the privacy warnings posted. He knew gammas would have seen his truck over a mile ago and reported that he was on his way. Not that the compound was a secret. It was officially a charity. It helped that two of the local deputies over in Asheville were wolf shifters.

"Don't you think it was a huge risk for my mom to take when she knew how dangerous it was to be with my dad?"

Ryker glanced over at the worried look Emmett wore. This had probably been bothering him a while. "No. Your mom and dad would have been naturally attracted to each other without definitely knowing why."

Emmett still looked confused. "But surely her need for safety would have overridden attraction. I mean—"

"It's more than that. The mating instinct for a shifter is a very powerful one. It can't be ignored, and sometimes separation can cause physical illness."

Emmett was quiet then, and Ryker wished he'd asked him earlier if he

BABY AND THE WOLF

had any questions. He had to get over himself and start thinking about his mate. He was going to get him settled, maybe stretch their legs—because exercise was good for the pup—get some of Dinah's food into him, then he had to tell him everything.

Ryker finally pulled up, and Emmett looked with interest at the huge house. He turned the engine off and smiled. He'd helped build it. Of course, it was a lot bigger now.

The forest stretched for miles behind it, and the huge cabin looked like it belonged amongst the trees. Wooden steps rose to two massive doors. Nearly all the windows at the front had their own patio area, so the shifters who were too traumatized to even think of going near the tree line could at least get some sun.

"It looks like one of those fancy ski resort hotels."

Ryker chuckled. "Might as well be in the winter." He hopped down and was around to Emmett's side to help him before Emmett had so much as gotten the door open. He made sure Emmett was on his feet and turned around as he scented Chrissy. She was jogging down the steps with a big smile on her face. She opened her arms wide and enveloped Emmett in a hug. He looked at Ryker, startled, but didn't seem to object.

"May called me. I was expecting you both. It's so good to meet you, Emmett. I'm Chrissy." She eventually let go and sent Ryker a knowing look. Ryker pretended he hadn't noticed, but he knew none of the shifters who could even hear Emmett's second heartbeat would say a word. When you lived in a world where hearing, sight, and smell were exponentially increased, privacy was jealously guarded.

Chrissy looked over Emmett's shoulder as she stepped back. "Emmett, it's Kai's first day as well. Come and say hi."

Ryker turned as he smelled a wolf shifter, and his world seemed to go very quiet. The young man smiled shyly at Emmett and returned the handshake Emmett offered. "Kai's not a panther omega. He's a wolf omega."

"And trying to get this pup to stop doing acrobatics." He rubbed his swollen belly ruefully and smiled at Emmett. "This is one of those days I wish I was an alpha. *Grr*." He grinned impishly. "Sorry I can't stay and chat

—I also have to visit the bathroom a million times a day." He rolled his eyes and headed in the other direction.

If Chrissy heard Ryker's heart stop beating, she gave no sign of it. "Let me know if you need anything. I know Dinah's got lunch ready whenever you are." She hugged Emmett again and walked back to the pack house.

Ryker swallowed, turned to grab Emmett's bag, and risked a look at him, knowing his plan of a talk later just got blown out of the water.

He started walking in the direction of the cabin, not even a little bit sure Emmett wouldn't go the opposite way.

CHAPTER SIX

EMMETT FOLLOWED RYKER, still reeling a little from how welcoming everyone was, hoping he might make friends as well as a new family. He'd met a few people in the different apartments in Asheville, but Emmett wasn't exactly a social butterfly. He'd been to one party, stood in a corner, and escaped as soon as possible. Katy had gone easy on him, but Mark had ragged him every day to go out. It wasn't that he didn't want to meet people; he didn't like spending other people's money, and until he got a job, he was stuck.

Ryker led him down a path that opened up to a small cabin. He unlocked the door, and Emmett glanced around. This wasn't some hotel-type accommodation. This looked lived-in, from the small laptop on the desk in the corner to the crammed bookshelves. He glanced at Ryker, who looked like he was about to be asked to walk the plank. "This is lovely. I'm assuming this is your place?"

Ryker's surprise was quite funny. "That's the first question you're gonna ask me?"

Emmett went over the last few minutes in his mind, wondering if he'd missed something. "Should it be something else?"

Ryker tossed the bag on the couch and nodded to the tiny kitchen.

49

"Let's sit down." Emmett's nerves ramped up, but he followed him without protest.

Ryker rubbed his beard. Emmett had seen him do that a couple of times when he wasn't sure about something. "I thought you might have questions about Kai." Emmett went to shrug because he really didn't know...*or maybe I do.*

But did he? Ryker had held his hand, for fuck's sake. He had set him on his lap. And that didn't include the whole night they had together. Emmett tried to swallow past the huge lump in his throat. Maybe it was different for wolves. "Is the baby yours?"

Ryker jerked back as if he'd been hit. "*What?* No, of course not."

"I know I've lived with humans, not shifters, but even I know what a trans—" But Ryker was shaking his head.

"He's not transgender. He's a male omega."

Emmett was very glad he was sitting down. "But a male *wolf* omega?" he asked very quietly and slowly because he had a feeling the answer was going to blow his mind.

"All male omegas can get pregnant, Emmett."

Emmett was silent for some time while that sentence pinged back and forth in his head. "You mean I could get pregnant?" he laughed, but it was in astonishment, not quite humor. "I'm glad I'm sitting down."

Ryker made an impatient noise and, standing, plucked Emmett off his chair and into his lap. "I can't have this conversation with you so far away." Emmett turned into Ryker, glad to hide his face but very glad to be held as well. What was it about Ryker that made him so content when his arms were around him? "Is this a shifter thing as well?"

Ryker nodded and wrapped his arms around Emmett. "So—" Emmett said hesitantly. "I—you, we have to use condoms?"

"It might be a little late," he admitted in a strangled voice. It took Emmett a moment, but then he pushed away from Ryker and stared at him.

"Are you saying I could be *pregnant?*" Ryker winced. "You are, aren't you?" Emmett shrieked.

"It's not just a possibility," Ryker said. "It's—I mean, you are."

Emmett blinked at Ryker very slowly. "I'm pregnant."

BABY AND THE WOLF

A short nod.

"But how do you know? I didn't see you asking me to pee on a stick."

"Wolf shifter hearing is exceptional. Alpha hearing even more so. I couldn't tell until I held you at your apartment, but I can hear two heartbeats. Yours and our baby's."

Emmett almost felt the color drain from his face. "Does everyone know?"

"No. They would have to be really close to you." He squirmed. "I'm pretty sure Chrissy knows."

Emmett fell silent. He slid his hand around to his belly. "But—stating the obvious here—I'm assuming I would have to have a C-section?"

Ryker visibly flushed. "I think the best thing would be for you to have a talk with Kai. Or Chrissy."

Emmett turned accusingly. "Is that why you brought me? To see Kai?"

"No," Ryker said. "He's new. I didn't know we had any pregnant omegas. I brought you here because we needed to have this conversation, and I thought it would be good for you to meet some other shifters. Plus, your roommate was on her way back. *Plus,*" Ryker said, "it gave me some time to work out what to say."

Emmett paused to think about that. "Wait, so you didn't know when you came to see me?"

"No, not until I held you."

"But it might have been a possibility?"

* * *

RYKER NODDED, wondering where Emmett was going with all this. Emmett pushed against Ryker's chest and stood. He glanced over at his bag and bent to pick it up.

"Emmett?" Ryker asked cautiously, not liking what he was seeing. Emmett looked up, and Ryker sucked in a breath at the distress in his eyes. "I know it's a shock," he said desperately. "But I have no intention of leaving you on your own. I can—"

"Let me go," Emmett said calmly.

VICTORIA SUE

"But—"

"No. This was what all this"—he waved at the cabin—"was all about? You left me alone for nearly two months. You only came to see me because my dad asked you to, and you only brought me here because you managed to knock me up." He laughed a little hysterically. Ryker took a step forward, and Emmett took one back. "Don't you dare touch me."

Ryker froze. He didn't have a clue what he'd done wrong. His wolf was snapping at him, ready to shift right there and then.

"I'm going to find Chrissy and talk to Kai. I won't be staying with you tonight." He was out of the cabin before Ryker could think of a reply. Ten seconds later, Ryker gave in to his wolf and couldn't have cared less about the torn clothes he left on the floor.

* * *

EMMETT JOGGED down the path with his bag. Furious didn't come close. He headed for the clearing and let out a shaky breath when he saw Kai walking slowly past the pack house. "Kai?"

Kai turned, took in Emmett's bag, and met his eyes. His smile was warm. "Like a drink?" Emmett nodded gratefully. "We'll go the back way. I'm not up to all those steps."

Emmett stuck out his elbow for Kai to hang on to, and they walked around the side and in through a small door. A smiling woman turned around from where she was stirring something on a huge stove. She beamed when she saw Kai. "How's my grandbaby doing?"

Kai smiled back at her. "Stubborn. I think he's too lazy to move. This is Emmett. Emmett, meet Dinah. Everyone calls her Nana, hence the grand-baby comment."

Emmett smiled shyly and helped Kai get settled in a cozy-looking nook in the corner of the kitchen. Dinah bustled and got him some orange juice and something that looked like a milkshake for Kai and put the biggest sandwich Emmett had ever seen in front of him. He looked nonplussed. Kai grinned and patted his belly. "No room."

Emmett grinned. "But aren't you supposed to be eating for two?"

BABY AND THE WOLF

Kai chuckled. "I wish." He paused and tilted his head, studying Emmett, and then he nodded to the plate. "Dig in. It doesn't bother me."

Emmett didn't look convinced. "I can't believe how much I can eat. I thought I was just a greedy ass all these years." He picked up the sandwich, which he had to hold in both hands. "I only found out this morning that I'm a shifter," he added when Kai looked puzzled.

"Wow." Kai sat back. "Bit of a shock, huh?"

Emmett nodded at the understatement because his mouth was full. He nearly groaned at how good it was.

"I got here this morning. My alpha got a new mate, and I was given my marching orders."

Emmett swallowed. "But surely *you* were his mate?"

"Nope," Kai said. "I was just the stupid fool who thought he was in love and assumed he felt the same." He sighed. "But I should have known. I felt better the second I left him."

Emmett paused, not entirely sure what he was supposed to say to that. "But that's good, isn't it?"

"If he'd been my proper mate, I would have gotten sick."

Emmett froze. "Sick?" His heart started fluttering like a trapped bird.

Kai nodded. "Some omegas can get physically sick if they are separated from their mate for any length of time. It usually only happens with omegas and strong alphas these days. And I was fine." He shrugged.

"What happened?" Because he had to try and sound normal, concerned. Had that been what was wrong with him in the last few weeks? He'd felt a million times better since this morning, even after all the shocks.

"My dad died in a hunting accident last year. I never knew my omega. The alpha took me in and said he was going to take care of me." Kai shrugged. "He did right up to meeting his new mate. Then I was made to leave."

Emmett looked at Kai's very swollen belly. "I'm stunned."

"Oh, he doesn't know about this." Kai patted his bump. "And he can't. There's a chance he could claim the baby. Because of the low birth rate, all pups are jealously guarded. I've been staying with a couple, Seth and Jesse, a few miles away, but there's not much security, and with the baby due, they moved me."

"But how could he take the baby?" That was horrific.

"I'm not mated. Wolf law. I have to have one to be safe, and don't get me wrong, I've had a couple of volunteers from the ranger service, bless them, but I don't want pity." Kai patted his hand. "Enough about me. How are you?"

"I just found out I might be...well, I am, I think. *Pregnant*, that is."

Kai beamed. "That's wonderful." He met Emmett's gaze. "Isn't it?" Emmett sighed, then, remembering what Ryker had said about wolf shifter hearing, looked around the room. Dinah was puttering about, in and out of the pantry. "I haven't been here long, but I trust her."

Emmett chewed his lip and told Kai the story of how he and Ryker had met. "That makes sense though," Kai said. "Meeting your mate often triggers a first heat. Or you can take something that will mimic one if a certain alpha wants you willing." He rolled his eyes and waved at himself. "I was eighteen."

"You're eighteen?" Emmett said. Kai shook his head.

"Nineteen now." Kai took Emmett's hand this time. "I'm guessing you're a panther shifter because I can't scent you?"

Emmett nodded. "How long have you got to go?"

"Nine weeks or so, and I can't *wait*." Emmett returned Kai's grin. "Take a bite of your sandwich, then tell me why you were hightailing it over here. I've never met Ryker, but everyone around here talks like he's God. As in an 'isn't he wonderful' way, not in a 'he thinks he's God' way. In fact, I'm sure when this omega called Jason finds out he's spoken for, he'll consider his life over."

Emmett sighed. "He's not spoken for."

Kai chuckled. "Well, I don't know how it works for panthers, but wolves only truly mate once. You're it for him."

"We're not mated," Emmett argued. Although, technically, he didn't know what that meant.

"Uh-huh. Did he drug you to bring on your heat?"

"No," Emmett said quickly. "I'm not happy with him, but I know he wouldn't do that. And don't ask me why because I have no idea." Emmett scrubbed his face. "And apart from an infamous one-night stand where apparently I was in heat, we've known each other for two days with a seven-week gap in the middle."

Kai grinned. "I feel like I'm watching a daytime soap. Did you bring popcorn?" Emmett chuckled despite himself, but then Kai sobered. He looked knowingly at Emmett. "I'm guessing you feel better already?" Emmett flushed, and Kai leaned forward as much as his belly would allow. "When a wolf meets his mate, it's like their body thinks they've won the lottery. If he was convinced you were human, it was his head arguing with his heart."

"Well, I don't know about a wolf." Emmett looked up, hearing Chrissy as she sat down next to him. "But he's been like a bear with a sore head for weeks. And I'm assuming you're the reason." Chrissy patted Emmett's hand. "Did he tell you about his mom?"

Emmett nodded. "He told me his father killed her because he was drunk and lost his temper."

"He was, but she was killed because she was a human." Emmett gazed at her in shock. "It's why Ryker would never have been accepted as the alpha of his old pack and why his father was so bitter. He swore off humans, which is why he tried to give you up. Dinah and I had a bet going that he wouldn't last another week."

Emmett blew out a long breath. Chrissy nudged him. "Eat your sandwich."

Kai finished the last of his shake, then winced. "I have to pee again." He got to his feet gingerly. "Don't leave without telling me. I need all the friends I can get."

"It will be good to go through this with a friend." Kai didn't reply, just left hurriedly.

"I'm heading that way," Chrissy said and stood up to follow.

"Is he okay?" Emmett asked, worried at how Kai casually mentioned an alpha could drug an omega to mimic a heat. Was that what had happened to Kai?

"No," Chrissy said. "Which is why he needs a friend. He's scared that whatever that bastard of an alpha drugged him with might have hurt the baby. Marco's bringing an ultrasound machine to check, but he's terrified there's something wrong, poor lamb."

"Is Marco a doctor?"

"He's a medic with the ranger service." Chrissy smiled. "And one of ours."

Dinah came over and fussed while he tackled the sandwich, told him pointedly there were lots of spare rooms and to come and see her if he wanted one, then left him be.

Emmett ate automatically without really processing everything he'd learned. His head was so full he wasn't sure how much more he could fit in there, and he scrubbed his face, stifling a yawn. He got up, grabbed his bag, and took the plate to the sink where he rinsed it. He was still trying to decide what to do when he headed outside and ended up back at Ryker's small cabin. He knocked, but something told him Ryker wasn't there. Sure enough, it was empty and unlocked. The laptop was still on the small desk and tattered clothes lay on the floor. He eyed the couch longingly as he yawned again but headed to the bathroom, picking the clothes up on the way. There were only two doors, and it was the second one. The first was a plain bedroom with just a bed and a nightstand with a book on it. He went to the bathroom and then, unable to keep his eyes open any longer, stretched out on the bed and pulled the blanket from the foot of the bed over him. He doubted it would take more than two minutes for him to fall asleep.

CHAPTER SEVEN

RYKER'S WOLF caught the strange scent as they got close to the boundary, but he wasn't immediately surprised because he was close to the edges of the tourist areas and he usually had to avoid hikers and campers. He wasn't especially keen on scaring some hunter into shooting him either. Even though hunting was banned near the parkway, they still got the occasional idiot, especially out of season in the more remote areas. His wolf paused, trying to identify the scent as a shifter or not. For a second, it almost reminded him of his old pack, but as the wind changed, he lost it entirely and decided that was ridiculous. His old pack was thousands of miles away.

He padded onto a rocky outcrop and lay down, going through everything he had done wrong and wondering how the hell he was going to fix it. He understood Emmett's anger; he just wasn't sure what to do about it. To be honest, he'd never expected to have a mate. That in itself was amazing, but a pup as well. Ryker's wolf panted, but inside he was smiling. He looked over toward the pack house. He couldn't see it this far away, and the whole point was keeping it as hidden as possible, but he knew what direction it was in. Knew what was there waiting for him. He got up and nimbly jumped off the rock and headed through the trees. It would be dark soon, but that hardly bothered Ryker. If he had a chance of fixing this, it wasn't going to happen if he wasn't there.

Ryker headed for his cabin. He wanted to get showered before he hunted Emmett down, and he let himself in. He knew someone had been in as soon as he saw his torn clothing folded neatly on a chair. Going very still, he heard the sound of soft, even breathing and crept toward his bedroom. The sight of Emmett tucked up in his bed, under the blanket his mom had made, did funny things to his insides. He pulled the door closed so he wouldn't disturb Emmett and hit the shower. Was it significant that Emmett had come back to the cabin to sleep? There were plenty of spare beds in the pack house, but maybe Emmett wanted to talk to him as well.

Ryker paused in toweling himself dry. Emmett could easily have come back to ask him to drive him back to Zeke's and fallen asleep. Ryker had been gone at least three hours. His heart rate picked up and his fingers fumbled tying the towel around his waist. Finally dry and knowing he couldn't put it off any longer, he opened the bathroom door and padded silently to the bedroom. Emmett was still asleep, but he'd turned over. Ryker stared at the blanket. He only had it now because Zeke had pulled it off the back of the couch and used it to staunch the blood pouring from his bullet wounds. Zeke had wrapped him up in it and taken him with him. Kept him alive until he could shift. It had taken a lot of washing to get the blood out, but he'd saved it because it was the only thing he had of his mom's.

Ryker quietly pulled out some clean jeans and slipped them on. He glanced back to the bed, only to see Emmett awake and watching him silently. "I didn't mean to wake you up."

Emmett shrugged. "You didn't."

"How are you feeling?"

"Shocked, confused. Undecided."

About me? Ryker heard the question in his head so loudly he thought he'd said it out loud. He walked slowly to the bed and sat down, watching Emmett carefully. If Emmett moved away, he would back off. Emmett watched him but didn't move. He didn't speak either.

"I want to help you all I can," Ryker said at last.

A tiny tilt to Emmett's lips gave him hope. It was almost a smile.

"I know I have to look at this through a shifter's eyes. Change my human perceptions."

"You don't have to do anything you don't want to," Ryker said firmly.

"What do *you* want?"

What did he want? Where to start? He wanted him here, in his arms, but he doubted he would get that. Would Emmett consent to mate him officially? He'd taken his knot unknowingly, but would he take his bite? "I want to be able to still see you. I don't expect you to want to either stay here or in the pack house. We have to tell your dad when you're ready, but it would be safe for you at his penthouse. I can provide shifter security. You just would have to stay out of sight once you start showing."

"It doesn't seem real," Emmett whispered.

Ryker stood, unable to sit and hear Emmett tell him he wanted to leave. "I ought to apologize. I should have known. I'm old enough to recognize an omega heat, but I'm obviously not wise enough to recognize an alpha one."

"An alpha one?"

Ryker nodded, completely miserable now. "You're beautiful. Everything about you called to me when I touched you in the parking lot the day you stepped out in front of my truck. I'd even noticed you in the bar. My wolf was trying to tell me even then, but I ignored him because I..."

"Because you thought I was human?" Emmett finished gently.

Ryker nodded.

"Come and sit down. You'll make my neck ache staring at you up there, and I'm lazy enough not to want to move."

Ryker gazed at him, not a hundred percent certain he'd heard correctly, but when Emmett patted the bed, he sat immediately. Emmett even inched a little closer. Ryker's gaze dropped to his hand. Lovely slim fingers that would fit so perfectly entwined in his.

"Once I kissed you, it was like there was no turning back," he admitted.

Emmett smiled. "You were careful though. You would have stopped if I had asked."

"It would have been enough if I'd have gotten to hold you, but the decision is yours. All I ask is if I can see you. I will respect whatever you decide." It would kill him, but Emmett was the important person here, not him. Not even his wolf.

"I like it here," Emmett said. "I'd like to stay a little longer and explore. Meet some of the other shifters. I suppose I want to know about my culture."

Ryker nodded eagerly, hope catching light in his gut.

"I want to get to know you." Emmett reached out his hand, and Ryker took it, cradling it carefully. "You make me feel safe, and I haven't felt that in a long time, but I need more than a bodyguard. I understand your protective instincts will be riding you hard, and I think—hope—that because I'm safer here, you can dial it down a little while we get to know each other."

Ryker could do that. He could guard his mate so stealthily Emmett wouldn't even know he was there. "It's my mating instinct, but whatever you need."

Emmett narrowed his eyes suspiciously. "That seems too easy."

"I feel like I'm getting a second chance," Ryker admitted. "I'm not likely to do anything to blow it."

"Well, we've got what, seven months to get to know each other?"

"Actually, a little under three now."

It took Emmett a minute. "Wolves are only pregnant for five months?" he choked out. "But humans are pregnant for *nine* months."

Ryker nodded. "She-wolves are generally around seven, but as I understand with omegas, it's the lack of room inside. Bears are more as well, but their omegas can shift."

Emmett was silent for a moment. "I never thought to ask that. To be honest, I didn't ask for any details, and I guess I should."

"Dinah can help you. She's the pack mother, and we have a medic as well, but he works for the ranger service, so he's not always here."

"Marco. Chrissy told me." Emmett yawned, then snuggled down again.

"Are you hungry?"

He shook his head.

"Then why don't you get some more sleep? I know it's early, but you have a bit of catching up to do, I'm guessing."

"Where are you sleeping?"

Ryker studied Emmett, trying to work out what he wanted to hear. "I was going to use the couch. It's big enough, and I've slept on there a few times. I won't disturb you, but I'd like to stay close in case you need anything."

Emmett didn't reply right away, but then he nodded agreement. "I'm going to go to the bathroom, then I think I'll take your advice."

Ryker grabbed a couple of bottles of water from the fridge and left them on the nightstand while he was in the bathroom. Then he went to make himself some dinner and a few snacks for the fridge in case Emmett was hungry later.

EMMETT FELT okay when he woke. He felt safe sleeping in Ryker's bed, pretty much like he'd felt whenever he was with him. The cabin seemed silent, so Emmett got up and went to the bathroom to pee and brush his teeth. He wanted a shower before he got dressed, so he pulled on a robe that must have belonged to Ryker. It was really big, but he loved the thought of being wrapped up in something Ryker wore. Emmett smiled at the thought of Ryker taking care of him. It seemed like Ryker did it without thinking. Instinct? *Mating instinct?* What exactly did that mean? Emmett wrapped the robe tightly, having to roll up the sleeves, much to his disgust, and found some thick socks that had been left out with the robe and guessed they were for him.

He walked into the living room and saw it was empty, then glanced over to the windows and the deck. He helped himself to some orange juice and carried the glass to the door, something in him urging him to step outside. He wasn't one bit surprised to see the large black wolf lying on the deck, head on its paws, and recognized Ryker right away. The wolf—*Ryker*—lifted his head and eyed him warily.

"It doesn't bother me," Emmett said, knowing it didn't. "This is your home, and your wolf is as much a part of you as the man is." He sipped his juice, hoping he'd said the right thing, and after a few seconds, Ryker laid his head back on his paws.

Emmett's belly rumbled, and he put his hand to it in embarrassment. Ryker lifted his head and made a sound like a sneeze. Emmett thought it was probably the equivalent of a laugh. Ryker slowly got to all four paws and watched Emmett calmly. Emmett returned his gaze.

"Your eyes are the same. A little more golden in this light, but I know it's you." He put out a hand, worried he might be treating Ryker like a dog, but Ryker took that as encouragement and came closer. He nudged Emmett's fingers, and Emmett's heart might have melted a little. Ryker pushed under his hand, and Emmett took the hint, stroking the thick fur down Ryker's head.

"Do you like that?" Ryker pushed under his fingers and came much closer, his body rubbing against Emmett's legs, so Emmett got even braver and scratched behind his ear, chuckling as Ryker twisted his head in encouragement for Emmett to reach some obviously itchy spots. "You'd better not have fleas," Emmett said without thinking, but the disgusted look Ryker sent back had him giggling.

Then he subsided. It had been a long time since he had laughed. "I'm hungry. Do you want breakfast?"

Ryker changed back so suddenly Emmett grinned.

"I guess that's a yes."

Ryker put out a hand, and together they went back into the cabin. Emmett tried to ignore the fact that Ryker was naked. And gorgeous. Had he mentioned how droolworthy Ryker was? Emmett snorted. It sounded like he was doing a mental diary. *Dear Diary, I met a gorgeous hunk of man today. Did I mention he changes into a wolf?*

"What are you hungry for," Ryker said in a low, gruff tone that went right to Emmett's knees. He wobbled, and Ryker immediately caught him.

"I think I need to lie down first," Emmett said breathlessly. Ryker's face flooded with concern until Emmett gazed at him with big eyes, and he smiled, catching on. He bent his head and nuzzled Emmett's neck.

"I think that's an excellent idea." Then Ryker swung Emmett up into his arms.

"I can walk," Emmett protested, half to himself, but having all of

Ryker's attention was bone-deep satisfying. Maybe he was more shifter than he realized.

"But why do you have to when I can carry you?" Ryker murmured back and walked into the bedroom, lowering Emmett to the floor and helping him take off the robe. He pushed Emmett back to sit on the bed and took off the socks. Emmett scooted back and stared hungrily at all the glorious muscles on display. And his cock. Emmett licked his lips, and Ryker groaned.

"You can't do that."

Emmett looked up until he had his own moment of comprehension, and slowly he licked them again. For a six-foot man of muscle, Ryker had an adorable whimper. It was also incredibly satisfying that he was having that effect on him. This mating instinct was incredible for his ego, and he felt powerful like he never had before.

Ryker moved closer to the bed, but Emmett stopped him just before he sat down. Standing there, Ryker was the perfect height for what he wanted. Emmett shuffled to the edge of the bed, his hands reaching up and skimming Ryker's hips until he clasped his ass and brought him a little closer. Ryker made another sound suspiciously like another whimper, but all Emmett's focus was on the beautiful leaking cock in front of him. He remembered how wide it was, how it had pulsed inside him, and he quashed the fluttering in his belly and the way his ass clenched in delicious memory. This time he knew exactly what he wanted though, and before Ryker got any ridiculous ideas about stopping him, he bent and fastened his lips around his length.

Ryker jerked. "Sorry," he gritted out as Emmett pulled back, a little panicked he would go too far, but Emmett hummed around the amazing taste and let the feeling of control settle in him. He adored that Ryker had reacted like that to his touch, but he clasped a hand around the base just in case.

Ryker groaned, louder this time, and ran his fingers through Emmett's curls. "Fuck, you're amazing," he said almost reverently. Emmett felt his own cock lengthen some more and warning tingles in his groin he tried to tamp down. Emmett hollowed his cheeks as much as he could and drew

VICTORIA SUE

back, swirling his tongue around Ryker's tip, then sucking hard and going down to his fingers. Ryker gasped and tightened his fingers in Emmett's hair, and Emmett moaned approvingly. Ryker had been a little less careful that time, and he liked the thought of his big, controlled alpha becoming a little more unglued.

He liked it a lot.

Emmett kept one hand on Ryker's cock as he sucked and laved. He teased with a gentle scrape of his teeth and was rewarded with a shudder and more precum on his tongue. He brought his other hand to Ryker's balls and gently rolled them in his hand, loving how the skin puckered with his ministrations. His own cock throbbed, but Emmett couldn't do anything about that. He was lost. Lost in how Ryker's body smelled of sex, of man, the heady taste, and the way Ryker responded to every touch. He felt Ryker swell under him, and he muttered a warning, but Emmett had no intention of stopping. A burst of cum hit the back of his tongue, and he swallowed frantically, moaning around the taste and helpless not to let some dribble out as more and more flooded his mouth. Ryker's fingers tightened again, and the zing of pain went straight to his cock and set off Emmett's own orgasm.

Ryker thrust into his mouth and yelled his completion. Emmett felt Ryker bend over him, and he slowed. He swallowed once more, but cum was all over his face and chin, and he let go, raising his hand to wipe himself, only for Ryker's hand to clasp his wrist. "You're fucking beautiful," he whispered and bent, kissing and licking Emmett's lips and throat and cleaning all the cum off his skin. The thought that Ryker was tasting his own release nearly set Emmett off again, but Ryker hadn't finished. He eased Emmett back down on the bed and proceeded to lick and kiss Emmett's cock until he groaned because he was hard again.

"Ryker," he protested half-heartedly. Ryker didn't answer, just lifted Emmett's ass in his big hands. Emmett blinked. "You're still hard," he whispered.

"That's because my body knows we aren't done." Ryker lined himself up.

"Don't we need lube?" Emmett asked, desperately trying to hang on to

BABY AND THE WOLF

some thread of sanity. Ryker shook his head and skimmed Emmett's hole with his finger. He raised it to show Emmett, and it glistened before Ryker pushed it between his lips and moaned at the taste. Emmett's cock jerked at the sight.

"Our bodies recognize their mate. Even though you are carrying my pup, we will still react like this to each other." And Ryker kept his gaze on Emmett as he pushed inside. Emmett couldn't look for long as the most glorious heat and fullness seemed to fill his body. Ryker stilled when he seemed to be as far as he could go, and Emmett whined, the pressure building up incessantly.

"Please," he begged.

"Please what, my mate," Ryker asked softly.

"Move," Emmett nearly shrieked, but his words were silenced as Ryker's mouth slammed into his. A second later, bone-deep pleasure hit all Emmett's nerve endings at the same time, and his body lit with heat in sheer ecstasy. Ryker lifted his head, and a definitely animalistic cry came from his human throat, almost as if he was staking his claim. Then he lowered his head, nuzzled Emmett's neck, and bit him.

Emmett reacted like he'd been stung, but his body turned the sharp pain into intense pleasure, and another orgasm barreled through him. He wasn't a hundred percent certain if it was possible to pass out with pleasure, but for once he didn't try and stop his body as it seemed to drift away.

CHAPTER EIGHT

EMMETT WOKE for the second time that day—okay, so maybe he hadn't been asleep—to the sound of Ryker's cell phone ringing. The loud grunt from the other side of the bed told Emmett that Ryker was as thrilled about it as he was, and he opened both eyes wide in time for Ryker to answer the call.

"Where?"

Ryker's voice went from sleepy to alert in a nanosecond. He nodded. "I want security. Wolves? Bears?" He swore and hung up. "I have to go. The scouts have seen a truck heading our way with a couple of hunters in it. Humans don't respect the signs, and we have some elk shifters higher up."

"*Elk* shifters," Emmett said in awe, although why he thought that was odd when he knew about panthers, bears, and wolves, he had no idea.

"They come here because elk hunting is illegal in North Carolina, and they are very rare. We don't want them to go extinct like tiger shifters, but a lot of humans don't care. They are very shy and don't really interact much with other shifters, but Shifter Rescue tries to keep an eye on them. Hunting is illegal on this stretch. The humans don't have cameras with them, they have .338 Winchesters."

"That's a gun?" Emmett asked, not having much experience with them.

Ryker pulled on his boots after his jeans. "Yes, but it's not really the gun, per se, but that you need a big cartridge because elk hide is tough." He pulled on a sweatshirt and grabbed his jacket and keys. "I'm going to send someone down to keep you company." He brushed a kiss on Emmett's lips.

"No need. I'm going to grab a shower, then go to the pack house." He swung his legs out of bed. "Be careful."

Ryker suddenly stopped and stared at him. Awed, he traced a finger gently around Emmett's collarbone. "It looks so good on you," he said huskily, then dropped his hand and was gone in an instant. Emmett rushed to the bathroom and leaned against the sink and stared into the small mirror above it. He'd always thought himself pretty unremarkable. Black, unruly hair he could never quite tame and gave up trying most of the time. Annoying pale skin that burned so easily in the sun and a nose that turned up a little at the end. He was used to looking washed-out most of the time, but this morning there was one thing that definitely hadn't been there the night before—the huge bite mark on the skin at the top of his shoulder. He remembered a brief moment of pain and the second orgasm that had followed. Dazed, Emmett went back into the bedroom, sat, and went over everything that had happened in the past twenty-four hours. The last couple of months, really. He'd forgotten a lot of what it had been like with his mom. The horror of living with Barry had replaced all that. He would have loved to meet his mom's family, but if what Ryker had told him was true, and he had no reason to believe it wasn't, he wasn't safe if they knew about him.

He had the feeling the mark on his neck was significant, but he wasn't exactly sure what it meant. He was hungry, but not in the ever-present gnawing way he had gotten used to over the past few years, but in the *ooh, let's see what delicious snacks are in Ryker's fridge* way. He needed a shower, but he was thirsty and went to the fridge to get some juice. Then he headed for the shower and took his time. It had been great meeting Kai yesterday, and Ryker had said there were some other omegas who lived here. The thought of having friends made him almost giddy, and he finished his shower, eager to start his day.

BABY AND THE WOLF

Emmett padded back into the bedroom and dragged on the only other pair of jeans he had brought, having expected to only stay one night, and wondered how he could get some more clothes or if there was a laundry here. There certainly wasn't a washing machine in the tiny kitchen. He borrowed one of Ryker's shirts, which was ridiculously large on him but covered the base of his neck that he wasn't so keen to show everyone until he knew what it meant.

He was still musing on that as he left the bedroom and walked into the kitchen. He stopped dead at seeing the man casually sitting on one of the kitchen chairs and then nearly threw up when he saw the large gun balanced on his knee.

"Fuck's sake, Emmett. How long does it take to get a shower?"

Emmett wanted to suggest Barry try it sometime and then he'd know, but his uncle's idle touch on the barrel kept him quiet. "What do you want?"

Barry huffed and tried to paste a hurt look on his face. Emmett didn't buy it, obviously.

"I can't come and visit my favorite nephew? That's hurtful, especially as I kept a roof over your head for years."

Emmett tried to think if he could get to the door without getting shot, but he doubted it. "We both know I worked off any so-called debt."

Barry scowled, then shrugged. "Get your jacket. We've got a long way to go."

"Why should I go anywhere with you?" And if to prove he wasn't stepping a foot out of the door, he walked to the table and sat down. If Barry had been surprised at his boldness, he didn't show it.

"I have a proposition for you." Emmett scoffed disbelievingly, and Barry merely shrugged. "You don't want to get back at the person responsible for your mother's death?"

"Is that Hannah or Josie?"

Barry shrugged seeming unsurprised.

"You mean it wasn't you?"

"Are you serious?" Barry said, and Emmett didn't think his surprise was faked. "I've been waiting all my life to get rid of my stupid bitch of a mother." He leaned forward. "Why do you think I kept you safe, huh?"

"Safe?" Emmett said incredulously. "You treated me like a slave." Realization slammed into him. "That's why I was never given proper food. You knew not having protein would make me sick and keep me dependent on you."

"It was the only way. You think I could have just let you wander about? Go to school? She'd have ripped you to shreds the same way she did your mother."

Emmett fisted his hands under the table. He meant the Panthera.

"I'm assuming you know all about panther shifters now. How the clans are run? Always down the female side. Your mother would have taken over when she reached twenty-one if she'd have wanted to, but what did she go and do? Fall for a fucking human and ruin everything. She wouldn't stay and fight, just fucked off. Then I found out about you, and there was another chance of getting the bitch out."

"I hate to point out the obvious, but I'm not female." Emmett tried not to shake.

Barry leaned over. "No, you're something even fucking better than that. You're a direct-descendant omega, and there hasn't been a male omega born in over five hundred years. The clan would be yours for the taking. No one would stand against you."

Emmett shook his head. "But I'm still half-human."

"Doesn't matter," Barry snapped back. "Omega trumps everything."

"How do you know I just don't shift?"

Barry scoffed. "Because of what Josie was. Not all females are omegas, but panther omegas always birth other omegas. It's in their DNA."

"Why is it so important though?" Emmett asked. He'd never seen Barry so animated. All the time he'd known him, he was a lazy slob. He couldn't believe he would shift into a sleek, powerful cat. In fact, he almost demanded Barry proved it, but he didn't want to give him any ideas. He'd seen enough of Barry's bullying over the years, and that was while he was still human without a set of sharp teeth and claws.

"Because I'm sick of her dictating my life. Did you know we get an

BABY AND THE WOLF

allowance?" He scoffed. "A fucking allowance like some kid when she's got millions."

"And why didn't you tell me?"

"You were a kid," he protested. "I had to keep you safe. Josie trusted me."

"You sure had her fooled, then." Barry looked amazed that Emmett would dare speak to him like that, and Emmett wasn't surprised. He'd been like a frightened rabbit when he lived with his uncle. But that stopped right now.

Barry smiled eagerly and patted the rifle. "You wanna live here, right?" Emmett didn't reply, but he didn't think Barry needed a confirmation. "Well, you need an advisor to handle things."

"You, of course," Emmett said dryly.

Barry nodded. "Win-win."

Emmett nodded and stood up, pretending to consider things. "So let me get this straight. You need me to get rid of your mother. Then you want me to leave you running things in return for which I can stay here?"

Barry nodded, but he narrowed his eyes a little, clearly understanding Emmett didn't seem that enthusiastic. "Panthers don't live together. You can live where you like. She has assistants, I can be yours. You would be paid, obviously. Hell, you wouldn't have to ask the humans for any money then. We just have to go prove to the clan who you are, then you can come back and rescue as many poor abandoned omegas as you want." Barry didn't quite manage to keep the derision out of his voice, but he tried.

"No," Emmett said baldly and sat back down.

Barry laughed and picked up the gun. "You don't have a choice."

Emmett smiled. "I'm pretty sure I do. If you shoot me, your only chance of getting rid of the Panthera dies as well."

Barry's fingers tightened around the gun, but then there was a knock at the door.

"Emmett, love?" It was Chrissy.

Heart hammering, he stood up. "I'll get rid of her." He couldn't risk she would be hurt.

71

VICTORIA SUE

But Barry just lurched to his feet and dashed to the back door. He was gone in another moment.

Shakily, Emmett went to let Chrissy in. He opened the door and was surprised when Chrissy roughly pushed past him.

"Who is it?" She inhaled, and a rumble came from her throat.

Emmett shook his head. "I thought you couldn't smell panther shifters."

Chrissy's eyes widened. "I can't. I can smell gunmetal and oil. Who was it?" She started pulling at her shirt to undress, and Emmett caught her hand.

"My uncle. Please, let him go." He pressed his lips tight and deliberately wavered a little. Chrissy went immediately into protector mode, and Emmett felt terrible for fooling her, but he couldn't live with himself if Barry got a shot off if she came after him. He told her what had happened. She nodded and got on her cell phone as they walked to the pack house.

"One of them usually stays human to man the phone if they need extra help." Emmett heard someone answer the phone but not what they said. Chrissy listened and then said, her voice a little uptight, "Can everyone come to the pack house for an update as soon as you get back? Yeah, tell him Emmett's fine and with me. We just had a situation, and we need to talk."

Emmett smiled at the reassurance, but he would be the first to admit he would rather have a certain alpha wolf with his arms wrapped around him right about now. They'd just sat down with a drink when the door slammed open, and Ryker, still fully shifted, loped into the room and right up to Emmett. He stuck his nose right into Emmett's belly, and Emmett—despite his fear of a few minutes ago—giggled and ruffled his fur.

Ryker nudged him, and Emmett, not really understanding what he wanted, stood and then waited patiently while Ryker stuck his nose in all sorts of places.

Chrissy barked out a laugh. "I'm going to get coffee for everyone while he makes sure you're in one piece."

As soon as she had gone, Ryker shifted and yanked Emmett close to him.

"What happened? Are you okay?"

Emmett nodded against Ryker's chest and breathed out a sigh of relief. "How did you know?" Had he heard what Chrissy had said on the phone?

"Because any situation involving you is important to me." Which wasn't exactly an answer, but he wasn't sure he cared about specifics. They stayed that way for a long moment until the sound of voices made Emmett remember Ryker was naked. He shouldn't have worried though, even though he really wished they were on their own, but Ryker caught the pants Chrissy tossed at him as she came back in, followed by two other men Chrissy introduced as Fox and Red. Red wasn't short for anything; he was named after his bushy red beard. He shaved his head completely, but Emmett guessed he would have red hair there as well.

"Tell me," Ryker demanded as he pulled on his jeans but then sat on a chair and lifted Emmett so that he was sitting on his knee. Emmett sighed, truly relaxing for the first time since he walked into the kitchen and saw Barry.

"My uncle Barry. That's what happened."

"I caught the smell of gun oil as I got to the door," Chrissy said bluntly.

Ryker wrapped his arms around Emmett, and Emmett told everyone exactly what had gone down and who Barry was.

"And I'm betting the hunters were there to draw us away from the cabin," Fox said glumly. "We need more gammas. I don't like the idea of panthers sniffing around."

Ryker sighed, and Emmett wondered what the problem was. They had space. Was it because there were fewer shifters?

"Why not ask Marco what's going on?" Red asked.

"Marco?" Emmett repeated. He knew he was the forest ranger service medic.

"He's a panther shifter," Ryker supplied. "But I'm not even sure if he is in the same clan."

"It wouldn't hurt to ask," Chrissy confirmed. They went through some more scenarios for security. Emmett got the impression they all wanted to say something but didn't.

Emmett and Ryker walked back to the cabin after the meeting. Ryker was quiet, and Emmett knew it wasn't just the problem with the panther clan.

"What is it?" Emmett said when they got inside.

Ryker glanced over at him. "I'm wondering if we need to move into the pack house for security." Which hadn't been what Emmett was expecting.

"There's more," Emmett pushed. "It felt like everyone was walking on eggshells a little. It seemed about more than Barry."

Ryker sat on the couch and pulled Emmett close. He captured his lips in a long, steamy kiss until Emmett just about forgot the question. He would be lucky to remember even his name by the time Ryker had finished ravaging his mouth. Ryker pulled away a little but then pressed his forehead to Emmett's.

"It isn't just the security issue," he admitted. "Chrissy, Red, and Fox have been pushing me into making this a proper pack."

"It isn't?" Emmett asked in bewilderment.

"Not at all. If we were an official pack, we would have to register it with the shifter council. We would need on-site medical facilities. Some sort of school even. At the moment, the omegas with children who stay here for any length of time are homeschooling, and Marco calls in once a week, but we have no emergency medical equipment other than what he brings. To be honest, we haven't needed it for the shifters because they heal when they shift, but the non-shifters and the kids too young to shift have caused a few hair-raising moments."

Emmett watched Ryker as he listened to him. He seemed uncomfortable. He didn't think it was the responsibility it would involve because Ryker never seemed anything but competent and in charge. He couldn't work out what the problem was though. Why was Ryker fighting this? "I don't understand why you wouldn't want it though. You're getting the extra space."

Ryker groaned and closed his eyes. "Because I'm a coward."

Emmett laughed. Not to ridicule him, but the thought of Ryker not being first into any dangerous situation was unbelievable.

"You wanna try that again, big guy?"

BABY AND THE WOLF

Ryker's lips twitched. "If we are an official pack, there has to be an alpha."

"I'm still not seeing—"

"Because I'm not one." Ryker moved away and stood up. "I'm a mixed breed. It's unheard of for a half-human to be alpha to a pack of wolf shifters. It just doesn't happen."

The retort "says who" was on Emmett's lips, but before he got a chance to speak, Ryker's lips were very firmly on his, and Emmett relaxed against him.

After another moment, Ryker pulled off and rested their foreheads together. "I'm doing this all wrong, and I'm not being fair to you at all." Emmett's heart started thumping, its heavy beat banging against his ribs. He'd changed his mind. Decided Emmett was too much trouble. For his sanity, Emmett pushed against Ryker, but Ryker didn't let go.

"Where are you going?"

Emmett huffed. "I'm not weak. Just because I'm an omega doesn't mean I can't handle it." But it would rip his heart out. He knew it would. And what about the baby?

"You're one of the strongest people I know." Ryker had a frown on his face like Emmett was being irrational.

"So, tell me then. I can go live with my dad. I would let you see the baby. I—"

"What the hell?" Ryker interrupted and looked at Emmett like he'd lost his mind. "You're leaving me?"

Emmett opened his mouth, then closed it again. "Aren't you going to tell me to?"

Ryker looked bewildered, and then he simply picked Emmett up and settled him on his lap. "I don't know where this conversation went, but—" He heaved a sigh. "If you left me, it would kill me."

Emmett had a moment to revel in that but then said, "But you said you were doing it wrong and you weren't being fair."

"And what in that sentence led you to me asking you to go?"

Emmett had another confused moment. "You didn't?"

Ryker grinned. It was quite an evil, self-satisfied grin, had Emmett had

75

the chance to really think about it. "I marked you as my mate. I guess I'm hung up on human timetables and feelings since I'm half-human." His grin widened. "But then so are you."

"And?" Emmett asked pointedly, failing at keeping the desperation from his voice.

"Mating is for life. Shifters don't get divorced. What I meant was, maybe should have had a ceremony with them all wanting to me to be alpha. That I'd done it the wrong way, not that I'd done it wrong in the first place. And I'm sorry I neither asked you nor made it clear what the bite meant, but in that moment at least I was very much the alpha claiming his mate." Ryker swallowed. "And I don't regret a second of it."

Neither do I. Emmett's heart still thudded. But his time it wasn't because he was afraid. "What does this ceremony involve? I mean, if just two people attend."

Ryker didn't answer with words. He used his lips, his hands, and his body. Very slowly and very tenderly, all Emmett's clothes came off. At some point, Emmett knew they went to the bedroom because he stretched out on the bed. Ryker was breathtaking. His fingers strummed and played Emmett's body like a maestro, trailing the length of his body, teasing his swelling cock with deliberate strokes and kissing his length. His lips were utter magic. The way they sucked, beckoned, and teased him to a degree of hardness he didn't think possible without exploding. He was mindless. Stroked, gentled, demanded to a completion he was at the same time oblivious to and desperately craved. He wanted Ryker's cock. Demanded in soft pleas and bucking motions until he thought he would go mad.

And the hard thrust of Ryker's cock into his hole wasn't enough, would never be enough, and he didn't know why. Delirious with sensation and crazed with lust, he felt Ryker move inside him until he swelled and he lowered his head to Emmett's. A combination of deep satisfaction and the inability to move. "I should have known the first time."

"What?" Emmett gasped out on the brink of something he couldn't name, wasn't sure he cared to name.

"I knotted you the first time. It will be like this between us whether the first or every time after that. My body has found its home in you. I'm here to stay, and I would kill anyone who thinks otherwise."

But Emmett's mind was swimming in lazy circles. He felt the need, even if he didn't grasp the words, and a deep satisfaction and completion he had only felt once before when Ryker had held him took him in. He didn't care about anything but the man who held him in his arms.

And making sure he never let him go.

CHAPTER NINE

IT WAS COMPLETE SHIT, but Ryker's phone woke them again. He sent Emmett a half-asleep, apologetic look and answered it.

Ryker listened a moment. "Get the team ready." There was a pause. "Then we'll have to manage without one." He scowled. "I don't care. What about Jesse?" He was quiet for a moment. "Louis?" But he winced the second he'd asked the question, then told whoever he was talking to he'd be about thirty minutes. He tucked the phone under his chin and listened for another two or three minutes. He sent a regretful look to Emmett as he pushed the phone into his pocket. "I'm sorry. I have to go."

"Is there a problem?" Emmett followed Ryker as he pulled on his clothes and stalked to the door.

"I told you I do the rescue work? Well, the park rangers found a cave with a group of shifter kids from a pack that was taken over recently."

"Kids?" Emmett said in surprise, fully waking up.

"They've gotten stuck in there, and if any of them are in the state of the omega coming to us, they're going to need a medic. The trouble is they don't trust us, and the rangers are worried the whole cave system is unstable."

"Does someone from their pack know them?"

Ryker shook his head. "No, these kids were held separately from the rest of them."

Emmett frowned. "How far away is the cave?"

"Twenty minutes."

"Can I come? I'll be careful and stay out of the way." He took a gamble when Ryker hesitated. "If I'm going to live here, I want to know what it is you do." He saw the flash of longing in Ryker's eyes and guilt stabbed at him. He still wanted to go though. "And I think the bite mark on my neck kind of qualifies me."

Ryker flushed. Emmett didn't want to score points. That wasn't what this was, but he was serious about wanting more than a bodyguard. "You promise to do what I say when I say it? And that's not me being a dick. I won't know what the situation is until I get there." He sent a meaningful look to Emmett's belly.

"Promise."

Ryker nodded, and Emmett grabbed a warm jacket. He was glad he'd remembered to bring his boots. When he was ready, Ryker came out of the kitchen with what looked like a sandwich. "Eat," he instructed.

Emmett obeyed, unwrapping the packet as soon as he got in Ryker's truck. "Tell me what I will see?"

"Rescue One will be on site in about fifteen minutes—Fox, Red, Chrissy, Liam, and TJ. We're going to pick Chrissy up on the way. The EMT–Marco–and two of the park rangers are there, but the kids are panicked, and there's an access problem apparently. We'll be able to see better when we get there."

"Are the park rangers yours?"

"Both human but trusted." Which explained a lot, Emmett supposed.

"Do you have a Rescue Two?"

Ryker nodded. "We can split up, but we only have one medic." They pulled up near the pack house steps a moment later, and Chrissy got in. She sent Emmett an approving look.

"How many kids?" Emmett asked.

"They're not saying," Chrissy replied. "There's one who's been talking a little, and Marco says he would guess eight or nine years old, but he won't confirm it. If he's been talking, it would make sense he's the oldest. From what we can gather from the pack, there seems to be around eleven kids unaccounted for, but we have no idea if all of them are here or not."

"Why are they in the cave?" Emmett asked. "Do we know?"

"They're scared to death and hiding," Chrissy said in disgust. "We think some asshole enforcer told the kids that the new alpha wouldn't let them live because of who their fathers were and they ran. When the omega houses got taken over—"

"What's an omega house?" Emmett interrupted.

"Well, according to what I was told, the alpha had four houses and he kept them totally separate. Each house had one enforcer and two betas to keep the omegas in line and to keep the younger kids out of the way until they started training, then they would go to a bunkhouse. If the enforcer deserved a reward, he'd let them take a turn with the omegas after the alpha was through."

Emmett paled. "You mean..."

Chrissy nodded. "Once the omega was pregnant with the alpha's child, it was a free-for-all nearly. No one could get the omega pregnant because he was already, but apparently this particular enforcer got his hands on the same drugs the alpha used to bring on their heats." She shook her head. "Omegas are like gold, and because of the low shifter birth rate some idiots think that makes them tradeable."

"What happened to him?"

"Riggs escaped in all the confusion while they were rounding up the omegas."

"Riggs?" Ryker snarled, and as Emmett glanced up at him, his knuckles whitened so much it was a wonder the steering wheel wasn't crushed.

"Do you know him?" Chrissy asked.

"It might be a coincidence," Ryker bit out. "My dad had a beta called Riggs." He swallowed. "He was a bully when I knew him, and he's the sort to progress to rape."

Emmett met Chrissy's gaze in the mirror.

"Is this the beta who shot you?"

Ryker nodded. "If it's the same guy. I have no idea what he's doing out here though. I moved because of Zeke, but my old pack is two and a half thousand miles away."

"Riggs was particularly vicious with Darriel," Chrissy said. "The omega we're getting tomorrow. Riggs tried to get Darriel to leave with him, and because he wouldn't, he beat him. He nearly killed him. He would have if Seth hadn't gotten to him."

"Is Seth one of ours?"

Chrissy smiled. "A hundred percent human and one of the bravest men I know. Jesse, his bear shifter mate, shifted and went after him, but he got away. They were too busy saving Darriel's life."

"He won't get far," Ryker promised.

Chrissy's glanced at Ryker. "I suppose Riggs is a common name."

Ryker's grunt was noncommittal.

"How is anyone these days allowed to treat people like this though?" Emmett asked. "You said omegas are rare."

"Yes, very. Panther omegas certainly. Wolves in particular went the other way and treated them like property. They're uncommon, but up to as recently as twenty years ago, wolf packs treated male omegas like mar-wolves," Ryker said.

"Mar-wolves?" Emmett queried.

"Because of gene dilution," Ryker said. "Shifters breeding with humans occasionally meant you would get a pup born that couldn't shift but wasn't an omega. They were called mar-wolves and often expelled from the pack."

"That's awful," Emmett whispered, his heart hurting for such an unjust system.

"And then the problem became worse," Ryker continued. "A lot of packs started reporting an increase in mar-wolves. The entire wolf shifter population took a nosedive, and many packs disbanded because they simply didn't have the wolves to keep them operational. So, despite being needed, omegas were blamed for the decrease in wolf shifters because they could never shift. Like they'd infected the race somehow."

"We know for sure that some packs have become creative in increasing their population," Chrissy added.

Emmett's heart started beating loudly.

BABY AND THE WOLF

"The pack we're getting Darriel from used male omegas for breeding. The alpha decided it was the only way he could get his own army, hence the omega houses."

"And some unscrupulous alphas will pay a lot of money to a pack to get their hands on one."

Emmett felt sick but was stopped from asking any more as they pulled into a clearing with two other vehicles; Emmett guessed they'd arrived. He got out slowly as Fox ran over to them. They were at the base of a sheer rock. There were two wolves prowling on the ground, and a man was lying flat on a ledge about twelve feet above them.

"The cave entrance isn't very high," Fox explained. "But we've had to pull away because we started a rockslide. There's a back entrance, but it's not safe. We sent scouts in, and the tunnel started crumbling, so they pulled out. We can't rappel down either for the same reason."

"Any contact?"

"Marco's got a little information from one kid, but he's scared. They won't come to the cave entrance, and we can't get to them. To be honest, I don't know how they got in there in the first damn place unless it was bigger and the slides have caused the problem."

Just then, an SUV joined the others in the clearing. Emmett's eyes widened when his dad got out and pulled his jacket collar a little higher. He looked equally stunned to see Emmett but recovered quickly. He walked over to them. "I was on my way to the pack house. What do we have?"

Fox briefly repeated what he'd just told them. Two park rangers appeared in what looked like climbing gear from the trees to the left. "The whole cliffside is unstable. There's a ridiculously small opening, we'd need a child to get through."

Ryker huffed. "Jesse?"

"Jesse wouldn't fit even if we could get him here, and he's in Asheville," Zeke said.

Ryker looked at one of the wolves who seemed the smallest, but that was relative. All the wolves were huge.

"How far away is the opening?" Emmett watched the wolf shimmer,

83

and a gray-haired man stood in its place. Red threw him a ranger's jacket and some pants, and he put them on quickly. "The actual access isn't bad, but then it narrows quite dramatically. The kids are petrified. I tried to test the walls, but any movement threatens another landslide. Fuck knows how they got in there. I think there are three kids, but I'm not sure. The little guy who's been talking to us is called Calvin, but he's convinced the enforcer is going to hurt him if he talks to us, and he's very reluctant to share anything."

"What about Fox?" Emmett asked quietly. "Won't he fit?"

Ryker followed Emmett's gaze to the wolf shifter and looked puzzled. "Huh?"

Emmett flushed. "Never mind," he hissed.

"No, what did you mean?"

Emmett squirmed. "It's just you said you had Elk shifters, so..." And Ryker's puzzled look cleared.

"It's a nickname because of his gray hair and his social life. If he isn't out patrolling, he's in some bar. He isn't a fox shifter."

"I can get guys with oxygen tanks, but they won't fit through," the ranger said interrupting the conversation and saving Emmett from embarrassing himself further. Then Emmett processed the problem.

"What about me?" Emmett spoke before he even realized he was going to.

Ryker and his dad both turned with identical looks of horror on their faces. "Absolutely not" and "No fucking way" were said in unison. Emmett ignored them both and looked at the park ranger who seemed to know the most.

"Will I fit?"

He looked warily at Ryker–who growled alarmingly–and nodded reluctantly. "You're about the only one who would, but even then it will be tight."

"You're telling me the ranger service doesn't have anyone else?" his dad snapped out.

"They do," the ranger confirmed. "She's on her way, but we can't risk a

BABY AND THE WOLF

helicopter for the same reason that the rotor draft might cause another land-slide. She'll be an hour."

"Which might be too late," Emmett said quietly.

"He can't even shift," Ryker said. "There's no way this is possible."

Emmett ignored him again. "What would I have to do?"

"Crawl through and find out why the kids won't come out. See if they're injured or if it's just fear."

Ryker snarled. "I forbid it."

Everyone's conversation died, and Emmett stared at him. He was tempted to ask exactly who the hell Ryker thought he was to forbid Emmett to do anything, but he met Ryker's eyes and saw the flash of fear in them. He walked up to Ryker—ignoring his audience—and reached up, cupping Ryker's face. "I couldn't live with myself if something happened to those kids and I could have helped."

"But you're—"

"Capable," Emmett interrupted, knowing his dad was listening.

Ryker's distress was palpable, and he leaned down and pressed their foreheads together. "I lied. I don't just want to see you. I want you here all the time. I couldn't cope with you being so far away, and I want you in my bed every night." Emmett guessed every shifter would have heard that, and he didn't dare look at his dad.

"Me too. So, let's get this done, huh? So we can go home?"

"That's bribery," Ryker huffed.

Emmett didn't reply, just made the "little bit" sign with his finger and thumb and turned back to the rangers. "Tell me what to do?"

"Actually," Red said, breaking the silence and looking at Ryker. "He can wear the new O2 guard. Impossible on a shifted wolf." Red didn't bother asking Emmett to change because bulking him up was counterproductive. It also meant he had very little on him in the way of protective gear except a hard hat. He just fitted a cross strap over his chest, pushed in a square, brick-looking thing but was incredibly light, and showed Emmett the small, folded mask. "It will only give you thirty minutes of oxygen, but nothing else will fit through there."

Red looked at Ryker. "Knee pads?"

Ryker shook his head. "Nothing that might get him snagged up."

Emmett was ready in a moment. He experimented with the oxygen, then quickly put it away to save it. "Do we know any other names?"

"Calvin's the only one who's talking. We're assuming he's the oldest, but he won't give us any more information."

The ranger jogged down from the ledge. "He says Sarah's gone to sleep and she won't wake up."

"Which could be lack of oxygen or simple exhaustion, Marco," Chrissy said, practically wringing her hands. Emmett glanced at the medic, frustration poured off of him. Emmett knew he had to do this. Red slid a water bottle into another pouch and stepped back.

Ryker stepped forward. "There's an open radio fastened to your belt. We can hear everything you say. You don't have to press any buttons to talk."

His dad was hopping from one foot to the other, clearly agitated.

Emmett walked up on the ledge. He wasn't worried at that point; even if it was narrow, it wasn't very high. They'd all agreed—much as he knew it was killing both Ryker and his dad—that he needed to go up alone to decrease the risk of a landslide. He was attached to a rope that Fox and Red let out slowly. He had a small, folded stretcher also attached to him that was just about big enough for a child when it was opened up. The entrance to the cave dipped quite sharply, and he crawled to the small opening in front of him. He stared in horror. He wasn't even a hundred percent sure he would fit. What if he panicked and passed out? He would cause more problems. Emmett took a deep breath and centered himself, then crawled nearer to the hole.

"Calvin? Can you hear me?" My name's Emmett.

What he got was a shuffling noise and a whispered "Uh-huh."

"That's great." He tried on the off chance. "Can you come nearer so I can see you?"

"No. If I move, rocks fall off the walls. One hit Sarah."

Emmett closed his eyes as a sick fear gripped him. He knew the guys were all listening, and the thought that Ryker was there gave him the bit of extra courage he needed. "I used to have a secret place to hide when I was

BABY AND THE WOLF

smaller," Emmett carried on as he shone the flashlight around the hole, but the passage banked a sharp left, so he couldn't see in. "Mom used to make me snacks, and I'd take a flashlight and some juice and pretend I was searching for treasure."

There was a silence for a moment, but then Calvin said, "Did you have to be quiet so the bad alpha wouldn't get you?"

Emmett's heart broke. Then he digested what Calvin said, and suspicion filtered in. "Calvin, did someone tell you to hide in here?"

Another silence.

"To hide from the bad alpha?" It was no good—he was going to have to go through. Not that there was an inch to spare. "Calvin?" he prodded.

"Yes." The whisper was so quiet Emmett nearly missed it.

"Was it Riggs?"

"Yes," Calvin admitted. "But we don't have any water left, and Sarah won't wake up."

"Is there just you and Sarah?" Emmett shone the light through, and apart from holding his breath when a couple of pebbles slid away, he managed to crawl some more.

"No."

Emmett shuffled further and tried not to think about how small the passage was. He couldn't even lift his head. "Emmett?" Ryker's voice was strained.

"I'm in the passage. I guess you heard all that?" He crawled determinedly. The roof was so low he felt it scrape his helmet. It was good that he wasn't claustrophobic. "Tell me when you can see my flashlight, Calvin."

"I can see it," Calvin said, a little hope lifting his voice. A couple more yards and Emmett was through. The drop into the cave was only another foot. Emmett slid through on his belly and knelt up, shining the flashlight. He smiled at the four faces that suddenly sheltered their eyes from the beam.

"Are you really going to get us out?"

Emmett glanced at the small boy, who he would have guessed at around seven was Calvin, and nodded. "Absolutely. Where's Sarah?"

Calvin nodded to another young boy with an older girl lying on his lap. Emmett tried to gently rouse her but she didn't stir. She had a huge bump on her forehead and a trickle of dried blood running down her face. She was breathing, which was about the only good thing Emmett could say. "Ryker? There are five kids including Calvin, who's the bravest young man I've ever met." Emmett let his words carry deliberately. "We have a girl, Sarah, who's unconscious and looks like she has a nasty bump on the head." He broke off and smiled confidently at them all. "It's yucky in here. I think we should all get out and go eat pancakes."

Four hopeful faces that lifted at that.

"There's a really good alpha who wants you all to join his pack." He kept his fingers crossed, hoping the shifter language would work. "I need someone really brave to go first and lead everyone out. All you have to do is follow the rope, and my friend Chrissy will get you all fixed up. Her mate, Dinah, is awesome. She makes the best pancakes."

"For real?" the little boy asked.

Emmett nodded. "I need to help Sarah." He fixed his gaze on Calvin while he unfolded the stretcher. "All you have to do is hold the rope and follow it." One end was tied to him, and the wolves had the other end. So long as the kids held the rope, they would get through.

Chrissy's voice came on the radio. "And I need some suggestions. I mean, what will I do if I tell her to make blueberry and you'd really like chocolate chip? What if I forget the maple syrup?"

"I'm real thirsty," a little girl–Ginny–whispered, and Emmett got out his water. The other two were Joshua and Mira. It was hard disciplining them to a few sips each, but he made it a reward for grabbing the rope.

"Calvin?" Brown eyes met his. "I need you to be the bravest and go first. I promise Chrissy will be at the other end."

Calvin nodded and grabbed the rope. It was torturous. Emmett kept the radio on and listened to the sounds of them all getting clear. He closed his eyes in relief as the last one got out.

"Emmett?" It was Ryker's voice.

"Sarah's unconscious but breathing," he confirmed.

"This is what we're going to do," Ryker said firmly. "You need to get

BABY AND THE WOLF

her on the stretcher, then tie the rope to it. You follow behind in case it gets snagged on something." Emmett felt one tug. Emmett clasped it and did as he was told. "Perfect." Ryker's voice was smooth and warm. "All we need you to do is get Sarah on the stretcher. Clip her in with the bands, and we will pull. I want you to keep ahold." It was so good to hear his voice.

Fastening Sarah was easier said than done though, but Emmett eventually got her secure. "Ready."

She was slowly pulled out the way Emmett had come in. The stretcher —small as it was—got snagged on everything. Emmett had to untangle it a few times. When he saw the entrance he could have cried, and with every inch he moved, he heard Ryker's voice encouraging him. He'd just freed the stretcher from the corner when he heard a distinct rumbling. "Pull," he yelled, and the stretcher yanked free. He was a second behind it and felt his hand grasped and pulled as the tunnel collapsed behind him in a shower of rocks and dust.

Then he was hoisted into strong arms, and Ryker simply jumped off the ledge. Emmett had a moment to experience the feeling of weightlessness before Ryker hit the ground with a thud and he was crushed protectively to his chest. Not that he minded.

"Emmett!" He lifted his head at the sound of Calvin's voice and saw Chrissy trying to hold him back. Emmett lowered his arms from Ryker and opened them as Calvin barreled into him. Calvin hugged him tight, and Ryker simply held both of them. His dad wasn't far behind and joined the hug. After a moment, when Ryker passed Emmett some water, he turned to Calvin, seeing him glugging his own. There were two SUVs ready to take the kids to the pack house. Marco was seeing to Sarah, but Calvin stuck to Emmett like glue. He glanced up at Ryker.

"Can Calvin ride back with us? I promised all of them Dinah's pancakes."

Ryker huffed. "You can all have whatever the hell you like. Marco is setting up a triage at the pack house, so let's get them all home."

"Emmett?"

Emmett turned to his dad.

89

His dad looked between Ryker and Emmett. He half smiled. "You were amazing, but I guess this means you're not moving in?"

Emmett shook his head but stretched out his hand.

His dad pulled him into a hug and whispered, "It wasn't what I was expecting, but he's a good man. I'll arrange for your things to be sent here."

Emmett sighed in relief. Causing problems between them was the absolute last thing he wanted. "Are you coming up to the pack house? I think we're going to need everyone."

"Try stopping me," his dad said fervently and rushed to help the shifters settle the kids into their seats.

Emmett felt a small hand slide into his and glanced down at Calvin's dirty but smiling face.

"You ready to go get pancakes?"

CHAPTER TEN

DINAH WAS ready for them when they got back. Mac and Amy, the betas that had helped out, rushed to get some additional beds ready. Ryker knew they had been expecting nine omegas, some with their kids. The adult female omegas wouldn't stay in the pack house, but would be in a separate house with their mates and kids, if they had them. Two didn't have any kids and three were hoping their kids were from the cave. Darriel, the badly beaten omega, was due to arrive sometime the next day after Marco had seen him.

Now, they needed more beds for the kids from the cave. Sarah was apparently going to be a pack mother and had—at nine—already helped an omega give birth. And then there was Calvin, who didn't seem to have anyone.

Emmett was amazing. If Ryker had expected Emmett to sit back after the cave rescue, he couldn't have been more wrong. Everything seemed chaotic, but Marco got the triage going pretty smoothly, while Dinah got the little ones seated with sandwiches and juice. The complete families went with Mac and Amy to their assigned rooms to have the chance to recover somewhere quiet. Emmett kept Calvin with him and helped where he was needed.

Sarah was awake and luckily old enough to shift. She'd just shifted back when her omega, James, got off one of the two trucks from their pack. Ryker smiled in satisfaction at the happy tears as Red got them to their room.

Calvin hadn't been withholding details when he hadn't told Marco how old he was. He genuinely didn't know. Apparently, he'd lived at the omega house for as long as he could remember. Chrissy said he could be as old as eight or nine, but to go with seven to be on the safe side. He was small and skinny, but that could be from a lack of food as anything else.

Calvin had refused to leave Emmett's side. When the dust settled, he was also the only kid who didn't have an omega present. Ryker hunched down when he got to where Emmett had Calvin on his knee, demolishing a sandwich. He was too thin.

Emmett brushed the too-long blond hair off the little scrap's bruised face.

"Cal told Chrissy that he doesn't have an omega, that the omega house he was in was for older kids who hadn't shifted. He says the bigger boys were taken from there as soon as they shifted for the first time, but if they got to twelve without shifting, they were taken somewhere else."

Emmett raised eyes awash with unshed tears. Ryker didn't have to tell him what that probably meant.

"And that there were two enforcers called Greg and David that…I'd say looked after them, but I think that's an exaggeration. Riggs was in charge."

Ryker squeezed Emmett's hand. He wanted to get Riggs if it was the last thing he ever did, but then he gazed at the mark on Emmett's neck, now visible since he had changed clothes, and he knew he had other priorities. "We're giving out details to surrounding packs to be on the lookout, but unless they use their real name, which is unlikely, or they are recognized, it might be difficult to catch them."

"What's the difference between them all? I've heard you say betas and enforcers."

"Gammas are usually regular pack members that take a turn helping with security. In my old pack, they worked exclusively for the pack, but in others they may have outside jobs. This varies, but the betas are generally the trusted advisors of the alpha. The enforcers were the full-time muscle if you like, but every pack operates differently." He paused. "Some packs would never allow non-shifters to join; some didn't differentiate, especially if they had other skills."

Emmett looked down at Calvin, whose head was nodding. He looked in danger of falling asleep holding what was left of his sandwich. Emmett took it out of his hand, hushed him, and pressed his head onto his shoulder. With a sigh, Calvin shut his eyes and relaxed. Emmett rocked him, but it was pretty obvious he was asleep nearly immediately.

"It suits you," Ryker said quietly. He couldn't wait to see him with their baby.

"Do all shifters shift for the first time before twelve?"

Ryker shook his head. "With wolves, some mixed breeds don't shift until they're teenagers. I was thirteen. Some don't shift at all. It's usually an indication they won't ever if they get to fifteen without shifting, and I've known some to shift as early as seven or eight, but that tended to be the alpha's children."

"But how would the pack know they weren't omegas? Unless it's just panthers that don't shift."

"Bear omegas can shift right up to labor. Female wolf omegas shift, but male omegas don't. Their insides are a little more complicated, and the possibility of pregnancy seems to shut off that ability."

Emmett nodded. "That makes sense."

"Every pack used to have at least one pack mother who could tell the pups that would be omegas, but from what Sarah told Fox, that was her job."

"She's *nine*," Emmett said in disbelief.

"Pack mothers are born with their abilities. She didn't realize what she was being asked to do, just knew it was something important. Sarah insists all the children in the cave are wolf omegas."

"And I'm guessing you're not going to tell her about the kids who weren't omegas," Emmett said weakly.

Ryker shook his head. "James, her omega, didn't realize what was going on. They were split up two years ago. I'm going to call a meeting. We need to decide what's going to happen."

"Can I come?"

Ryker cupped Emmett's face. "I wouldn't have it any other way, but Dinah says you can lay Calvin down in the kitchen. In case he wakes up, I don't want him hearing any of this."

Emmett nodded, and Ryker lifted Calvin, carrying him, still fast asleep, to the kitchen next door where Dinah had a small cot for him to lie on. Emmett watched as they got him settled.

"I'll stay with him," Dinah promised.

All of the rescue team filed into the large room with Fox, Red, and Liam. TJ came in with some coffee, water, and juice, and in another moment, Chrissy and Zeke joined them. Ryker sat at the head of the table with Emmett on his left.

He glanced at Chrissy as she sat down. "What do we know so far?"

"Of the five kids in the cave, only Calvin hasn't been identified. The problem is there are still at least four omegas missing, but I think that figure may easily double. No one but the gammas, who have disappeared, know which child goes with which omega since we don't have both of them to scent."

"What do you mean by scent?" Emmett asked because he was sure it was significant the way Chrissy had said it.

"We wolves can tell blood ties by scent," Ryker explained. "A father and son, for instance, or siblings. As some packs still don't register birth, it's accepted by the shifter council as official identification for a child until to a pack naming after they shift."

"Their what?" Emmett said, looking perplexed.

"All shifters belong to a pack if they are named as such by the alpha. It gives them a level of protection, rights. They share equally in the riches of the pack, even if they are unable to contribute financially or physically. It's a little like a pension if you will. The pack will always take care of that shifter, but until that naming, they stay with the omega or their sire, even if that wolf got expelled. Naming meant that the whole family didn't have to leave unless they wanted to, but naming can never be done before shifting."

"But what about the non-shifters?" Emmett asked.

Chrissy shook her head. "Which is why omega wolves don't have protection. They're not counted as official pack members."

"It's something a lot of us have tried to get the shifter council to change, but they're dragging their feet."

"But why?" Emmett asked, obviously bewildered.

"Because of the population being threatened. For years that has been their main focus," Red answered.

"So you're telling me that this council is willing to turn a blind eye to essentially farming children because of their precious population?"

The room was quiet for a moment, and then Ryker said, "We're trying to get them to listen, but it's...problematic."

"Calvin could belong to one of the missing omegas or none of them," Chrissy said, clearly trying to change the subject. "The enforcer who hurt Darriel has vanished. Seven gammas are dead. At least five other adolescents, maybe teenagers, are missing." She paused. "And I have seventeen official requests to join your pack."

Ryker's head shot up, and his eyes narrowed. "And I'm assuming you told them this wasn't a pack?"

Red scoffed, but Ryker ignored him. "Well?"

Chrissy just arched an eyebrow.

"The thing is," Fox said calmly, "this *is* a pack. You're more of an alpha than half of the ones I've known. We're all loyal to you. We treat you as our alpha because you put us first and look after the needs of everyone. If that's not an alpha, I don't know what one is."

"The land doesn't belong to the pack," Ryker ground out.

"Well, if that's the only thing stopping you, I can alter that today," Zeke said mildly. "It's in an LLC at the moment, but that's easily rectified."

Ryker gazed at Zeke. "You know that's not the only thing that's stopping me." He sighed. "What difference does it make? We would still do what we do."

"It creates belonging," Chrissy said. "It still means we can rehome where necessary, but some of us enjoy having this as our home base. At the moment, half your rescue organization is elsewhere, which was part of the problem today. And the reason they were elsewhere is mainly because those shifters with families need somewhere to access schooling. If we were a pack, we could have a proper clinic instead of borrowing Marco from the ranger service. We could attract wolves who can provide child-care, education. It doesn't mean we can't rescue shifters. I think it means we could do it better. And," she said pointedly, "we could name pack members."

Chrissy looked at Emmett, then back at Ryker, and for a second, Ryker didn't get it. Then understanding hit him like a brick. She was right. Where would their pup go to school? What if Emmett wanted a scan? What if something went wrong? Shifters in the main house needed little medical attention, but Emmett needed tests to see what was wrong anyway, and the last thing Ryker wanted was for him to have to go two hours into Asheville.

His skin went cold. Emmett couldn't make that journey when he was five or six months pregnant. What if Zeke and Emmett thought Emmett would be safer in Asheville? Then, what if Emmett decided he ought to stay there for the baby?

He looked over at Zeke, and Zeke nodded approvingly. Ryker chewed his lip. Were they right? Was he behaving like an alpha? He supposed so. The compound had always been his responsibility; likewise, the shifter rescues and the wolf discipline that followed. Zeke never got involved in that side of the business. He glanced around at his team as he called it. Chrissy and Dinah lived at the pack house, obviously, as did Fox and Red, but neither of them had family. Liam stayed during the rescues and went to his pack over in Sapphire the rest of the time. TJ had a family in Charlotte covered by the Danville pack. The alpha there was getting ready to retire, and his son was a bit of a hothead, but Ryker didn't have any problems with him. Marco was a panther shifter and lived near Asheville. The real problem was that Ryker wasn't officially recognized as alpha, which could easily happen.

"Is this what you all want?"

They all nodded.

"I'd have to transfer, and Ginny would need to look into schooling, but I know she's wanting to live somewhere else, especially since the twins were born," TJ said.

"One of the seventeen applications comes from a wolf shifter that ran the small school in the Mills River pack," Fox said.

"That's not necessarily a recommendation," Ryker said dryly.

Chrissy shook her head. "We haven't had much time to talk, but leaving the pack wasn't either easy or often not an option. He might not have had a choice."

Ryker nodded. "Let me have a few days to think about it."

They broke up, and Ryker glanced over at Emmett, about to ask him if he was hungry, when they all heard a scream from the kitchen, followed by a wail that got louder. Emmett shot out the door, and Ryker followed. Calvin was crouched back on the small cot, tears streaming down his face. Emmett widened his arms as he sat down, and Calvin nearly threw himself at him. It had been a nightmare, and when Calvin had calmed down a little, he told them he had dreamed the ceiling had fallen down in the cave and they were trapped.

Ryker leaned over and stroked the pup's head. He didn't want to frighten him, but he also knew Calvin was a wolf and they responded to touch. He wanted Emmett to get some rest, but he didn't know what to do about Calvin.

"Don't leave me."

Emmett shot a pleading look at Ryker.

"Okay, buddy." Ryker hunched down. "You can come and stay with us tonight, but you gotta hold Emmett's hand and walk next to him. He worked hard getting you all out of that cave, and you're a big strong pup that doesn't need carrying."

Emmett opened his mouth, and Ryker was sure that he was going to protest, but Calvin nodded and stood. He looked cautiously at Ryker. "Are you my new alpha?"

Ryker smiled at the little guy, but before he could say anything, Calvin rushed at him. He just got his arms untangled as Calvin cuddled in deeper. Emmett looked surprised, and Ryker understood how human kids would think he was scary, but shifter kids were different. It was in their DNA to look to their alpha for protection.

"You might have your own omega looking for you," he hedged.

Calvin seemed to consider that. "You're never gonna make me go back there, are you?"

Ryker shook his head. "No, buddy. We're still searching for your omega, but whatever happens, you would never go back there."

Calvin sniffed and pushed against Ryker even more. "I've never had an omega. Why can't Emmett be mine? He hasn't got a pup."

Ryker shot an agonized look at Emmett, who put his hand up to cover his mouth as if to stop a cry escaping. They were still talking to the pack members. They had no idea if Calvin had a family. "How about this? If we find your omega, we ask them if you both want to live here?"

Calvin didn't seem sure, but he nodded, and Ryker knew he would have to accept it. He had no idea what else to say anyway. He hugged Calvin for another moment, then solemnly clasped Emmett's hand and took Calvin's in his other. He didn't mind Calvin being there, but Ryker wasn't getting relegated to the couch.

An hour later, everyone had settled down. Ryker commandeered the large room downstairs that doubled as a bedroom when it was crowded. The cave rescue had overshadowed the fact they still had the Panthera and Emmett's maniac uncle to deal with, and security-wise he didn't want Emmett in a cabin close to the tree line. Calvin had happily had a bath and was now seated at the small table Ryker had taken from the kitchen, coloring.

"They're all underfed," Emmett said quietly and wrapped his hands around a cup of peppermint tea. "Covered in bruises."

"There's no ID for any of the omega kids."

"None at all?" Emmett asked in surprise.

Ryker shook his head and sipped his coffee. "No, remember what I told you? It's only needed if the shifter's going to interact in the human world. You'd be surprised by the number of humans living off the grid these days, never mind shifters."

Emmett seemed to think about that. "What was it at the meeting? There seemed to be something no one was saying." He rested his hand on his belly eloquently.

Ryker stared at the table for a long time before he answered. He owed

BABY AND THE WOLF

Emmett this. "One of the reasons my dad lost the pack was because of me. Mixed breeds can't be alphas usually. If I had been able to become alpha, we would have been less likely to get challenged. Mom—"

"Whoa," Emmett interrupted. "In what reality is being born to mixed parents your fault?"

Ryker opened his mouth, then closed it again. He'd never actually... Ryker let the indignation on Emmett's face warm him. "I suppose because I had it rammed down my throat for so many years. Even when I shifted and grew another eight inches in the space of a year, it didn't matter. I guess I was used to being blamed." He took a breath, feeling like something that had been weighing him down for years was suddenly so much lighter.

Emmett put out his hand, and Ryker immediately clasped it. "Is there any other reason apart from that?"

Ryker barked out a laugh. "I don't know whether the council would ratify a pack with a mixed-breed alpha."

Emmett frowned. "And why do they matter?"

"They're like the shifter governing body. The only time they really interfere is if shifters are doing something that threatens discovery by the humans. If shifter law is broken, it's usually handled at the pack level. Their main priority is saving our species." He took Emmett's hand. "You do know I don't agree, don't you? But it also means they may ratify the pack but not me. Another alpha could simply take over. I wouldn't even be challenged."

Emmett paled a little, but Calvin tugged his arm to show him his picture. Ryker refilled his milk and Calvin looked up to thank him very politely, then returned to his coloring.

"One thing that amazes me is that the shifters have managed to keep this from humans for so long."

"We have lots of motivation. Genetic experimentation, conscripted super soldiers. The list is endless."

Emmett shuddered. "I can imagine."

"I'd like you to see Marco when he's finished checking the kids. He'll be back with Darriel tomorrow." Ryker stepped closer and cupped Emmett's cheek. Emmett leaned into the touch.

"Having a full clinic here would be a good idea," Emmett said. "Are you worried you will run out of space?"

"I need to talk to your dad about the land deal he is doing." Ryker stroked a thumb up and down his cheek almost idly as if he wanted the closeness. "There's a farmer whose land butts right up to our western edge. It doesn't have the park access, but it wouldn't matter because we do. It would give us double what we have, which means we would have room for those who want to stay permanently and those who are temporary."

There was a knock on the door a moment later, and Calvin jumped. "It's okay," Ryker said and got up. It was Zeke. Calvin crept up on Emmett's lap and hid his face. "I'll go make sure Marco has everything he needs," Ryker said immediately, knowing Emmett and his dad needed to talk.

Zeke grinned. "Not necessary for me unless Emmett—"

"No, I'm good," Emmett said, then after a second followed it with "Dad."

Zeke stared at him for a long second, then smiled. "I just want to say one thing—well, two."

Emmett waved at the chair. "Do you want a coffee?"

Zeke shook his head. "I have to get back. There's a board meeting tomorrow I can't miss if we're going to purchase that land in Tennessee." Ryker rolled his eyes, and Zeke grinned. "I trust Ryker, but I want to make it clear right now if you ever need a home, you will always have one with me."

Ryker tried and failed to swallow the growl that came from his throat. Not that he really cared. Let Zeke try and take Emmett and he would show him exactly who the alpha was.

"Thanks, Dad," Emmett said softly. "Why don't you sort out what you have to do and then come back for the weekend? I want to get to know you too."

Zeke nodded. "I'd like that." He glanced at Ryker. "Walk me out?"

Ryker met Zeke's eyes and pushed off from where he had been leaning against the wall. They both walked into the corridor.

"I've made a call to the lawyers. I need a pack name."

BABY AND THE WOLF

Ryker huffed. "I said I needed twenty-four hours."

Zeke looked amused. "There's no way the logistics of not having a medical center and a school here haven't occurred to you."

"You know?" Ryker blurted out. "Emmett told you?"

Zeke stared at Ryker for a moment. "I was talking about the way your mate seems to have gotten very attached to the little guy in there and vice versa. What are you talking about?"

Ryker swallowed. *Shit.* What the fuck did he say? "Emmett's right. It would be good for you to come up for a few days. Get to know him." He waited for Zeke to call him on his bullshit, but after a moment, he just nodded.

"Okay. I'll see you Friday. I'm having May open accounts in your name. You'll need a lot of supplies. Let me know who you need to be on the payroll and I'll take care of it."

Ryker nodded and stuck out his hand. It was a human thing, but it felt right with Zeke. "Thanks. Your support means a lot." He didn't specify whether that meant for his pack or his mate, but he didn't think he needed to. Zeke didn't charm investors by being stupid.

Zeke clasped his hand briefly and then jogged all the way to his car.

A pack? Every day growing up, his dad had told him what a failure he was. How he would never be an alpha, like it was his fault he had been born. And for a long time, Ryker had believed him, until a certain omega had wormed his way into Ryker's life and put his faith in him. Maybe it wasn't so impossible after all.

CHAPTER ELEVEN

NEARLY TWO WEEKS LATER, Emmett stood with Ryker watching the helicopter land as Chrissy joined them. Five broken ribs, a ruptured spleen, and a punctured lung had taken longer than expected for the undernourished non-shifter to heal, but at least the new alpha of the Mills River pack hadn't kicked Darriel out before Marco had said he was ready.

"How does he afford this?" Emmett murmured half to himself.

"Your grandparents had a lot of money," Ryker said, "but I happen to know Zeke made his own fortune before he was left theirs."

Chrissy nodded. "May once told me your dad took a small inheritance from his grandfather and gambled with it on the stock market. It gave him a startup, and that's how he got into funding low-income housing."

"Ethically," Ryker stressed when Emmett must have telegraphed doubt. "His brand of cheap but reliable hit the right notes at a time when a lot of the bigger cities were stuck with overcrowding, so his ideas blew up. He now has a reputation that a lot of investors want a part of, and consequently when he needed to borrow a helicopter, people generally fall over themselves to help."

Chrissy chuckled. "Doesn't he have his own?"

VICTORIA SUE

"I'm guessing it'll be next on his list," Ryker said. "Thing is, though, he immediately jumped in to help when Marco said Darriel being in a truck and getting up to the pack house without causing him a great deal of pain wasn't possible. Even an ambulance would have problems on our roads."

Emmett watched as the engine cut and the rotors stopped spinning. He was really glad to hear that his dad had a good reputation. He hoped it meant the news they were going to give him this weekend went down easier.

Zeke was sitting next to the pilot and jumped out first. Head down, he got to the side door as it slid open. Marco was out next. Emmett heard a sharp inhale from Chrissy as they both helped the third young man down. Emmett was a ways back, but even he could see how gaunt Darriel was. It was a wonder he was standing.

"He might look worse than it is. He's a wolf, don't forget," Ryker murmured. "What might kill a human without medical intervention, even in an omega that can't shift, would heal given time."

Emmett shook his head briefly, but he didn't argue, and to be honest, he was pretty sure Ryker didn't really believe it anyway. The amount of abuse the young man had suffered even before the beating from a few weeks ago was horrific, and he had many badly healed injuries. Zeke had a very careful hold of one side and Marco the other. They approached Ryker and Emmett slowly, Darriel's eyes cast down after a quick glance.

"Why is he walking?" Emmett asked. "He should—"

"I assume he insisted," Ryker said. "I don't like it either."

Darriel paused as soon as they got eight feet away from him. "Alpha," Darriel murmured and shook off Zeke's and Marco's support. Emmett didn't realize what he was about to do until he half lowered, half collapsed to one knee. He'd seen some of the new wolves try and do this with Ryker, and Ryker had explained that he didn't want or need traditional obeisance.

"Old-school and definitely not something I'm interested in. He would have gotten down on both knees if I let him. Wolves who can shift do a similar thing but in wolf form. They lie prone to show me their wolf submits to mine. I don't need that either."

104

BABY AND THE WOLF

Yes, Emmett knew Ryker wanted loyalty, of course, but not this. He'd worked incredibly long days over the last two weeks trying to pull things together. Ryker jumped forward, catching Darriel's arm to stop him. He very gently took Darriel's hands in his.

"Your respect is acknowledged. Welcome to the Blue Ridge pack."

Emmett shot Ryker an approving glance at the name and happily accepted the squeeze from his dad as they watched Chrissy and Marco help Darriel inside. Zeke sighed and followed them in. "Marco told me it's only because he's a shifter that he's even alive."

Emmett understood how he felt. Even though Darriel would never shift, it meant he had withstood more than most.

Emmett squeezed his arm. "How about you come in for some coffee and we'll catch up?"

Zeke shot him a considering glance. Emmett deliberately didn't raise his hands to cover his bump. He was wearing a loose-fitting shirt and it was only noticeable if someone touched it.

Like a certain alpha did this morning. A wave of heat stole over Emmett, and he turned before his dad noticed. Calvin being there most of the time made it difficult to grab some alone time. It was amazing how sneaky Ryker was learning to be.

Ryker got himself and Zeke coffees, then deliberately put a glass of milk in front of Emmett. Emmett rolled his eyes but glugged it happily, much to his dad's obvious amusement. He lowered the glass and listened to them discuss pack security.

"Dad?"

Zeke turned, his face awash with pleasure at the name.

"I'm pregnant."

Unfortunately, Zeke had just taken a mouthful of coffee. He tried to swallow and inhale at the same time. It took a few minutes for his lungs to sort out the difference between oxygen and liquid while Ryker rather forcefully thumped him on the back. His dad held up a hand to stop Ryker. "Stop, or I'm going to have a few cracked ribs myself."

Emmett bit his lip. He hadn't meant to blurt it out like that. "I'm sorry."

VICTORIA SUE

But Zeke stood up and walked around Emmett's side of the table, pulling him up and into a firm but gentle hug. "I'm so pleased for both of you." He kissed the top of Emmett's head and put out a hand, which Ryker shook. "When are you due?"

Emmett's face flamed. He just realized he hadn't thought this through and shot a desperate look at Ryker. Ryker just folded his arms helpfully and raised an eyebrow. *Asshole.*

But Zeke let Emmett go carefully and stood back, gazing in shock at Emmett's belly. Pressed against him, it would have been obvious. "Don't tell me," he said weakly.

"We'll let you know after Marco does a scan," Emmett said, but he wasn't sure if that was better.

Chrissy came in after a moment and reported Darriel was settled. Then all three of them started discussing the Tennessee land deal. Apparently the problem was they needed someone to run the place who wouldn't be intimidated by the closest pack. Zeke had bought the land that the pack generally helped themselves to and they weren't keen on sharing, even when it hadn't been theirs in the first place.

Emmett excused himself to go see Darriel. He knocked cautiously, pleased to see Marco didn't look worried when he opened the door. Marco was just gathering his equipment together and turned to Darriel. "Call me if you need anything."

Darriel nodded and dropped his gaze to the bed. Emmett came in and closed the door behind him as Marco left.

"My apologies, alpha-mate."

Emmett smiled and pulled up a chair. He was tempted to sit on the bed, but he didn't want to hurt Darriel by accident. "Emmett," he said and covered Darriel's hand with his own. Darriel tensed but didn't pull away. "And I have no idea why you're apologizing."

Darriel was silent for a moment, and Emmett studied the frail but stunning man. Darriel's hair was as black as Emmett's, but while his was a wild, unruly mess most of the time, Darriel's long, silky tresses were gorgeous. His pale brown skin would normally be warm, Emmett guessed, but it looked almost ashen at the moment, made stark by his prominent cheekbones and huge golden-brown eyes.

Emmett grinned. "You're gorgeous. I am so relieved Ryker met me first."

Darriel's lips parted in shock, but he still made no sound. Emmett forged on, hoping he wasn't making things worse. "I'm new as well. New to being a shifter." No, that didn't sound right. "I mean, I only found out I'm a shifter after I got pregnant." Emmett shook his head. "No, I mean I *was*, but Ryker told me both at the same time. I'm a panther, and he thought I was a human." Darriel just stared at him. "I'm making this worse, aren't I?"

Then, unbelievably, Darriel giggled. It was only brief and not exactly a full-on happy-face reaction, but Emmett would count it as progress.

"You're pregnant?" Darriel asked shyly.

Emmett beamed. "I'm still wrapping my head around everything, and I can't believe it, but yeah. Nine weeks." He flushed. "I've even got a bump, and not one due to the colossal amount of food I'm eating." He tilted his head. "Are you hungry? I was thinking of getting a snack, but I can totally go somewhere else to eat it."

The knock at the door surprised them both. Emmett got up to open it to see his dad, and he stared. "Did you need me?" Then he looked down at the tray—fruit, chips, sandwiches.

"Dinah was busy, so I thought I'd help." He thrust the tray toward Emmett and turned and left, quickly closing the door behind him.

"He's human," Darriel said curiously. "He was in the helicopter."

"He's my dad," Emmett explained. "But I only found that out a few weeks ago as well." He set the tray down on the table so they could both reach.

"You've had a busy few weeks, then," Darriel said hesitantly.

Emmett nodded and chose a banana. "What I really wanted to do was ask if there was something I can do to make coming here easier?" He put the banana down when he saw the sheen of tears Darriel tried to hide. Reaching for Darriel's hand again, he stayed silent a moment, and Darriel entwined his fingers with Emmett's.

"Your dad told me in the helicopter this place is different." He didn't sound so sure though.

"From what Ryker tells me, packs are supposed to be big families, not prisons." Emmett winced. "We're still waiting to hear from the shifter council for them to agree to make this one official."

"Why wouldn't they?" Darriel asked curiously.

"Because Ryker is mixed. His mom was fully human." He waited for any reaction from Darriel, but he only nodded. Emmett guessed Darriel was used to being treated like *less* because he was different. He wasn't likely to have a problem himself.

"It wasn't so bad for some of the regular wolves. It was just that we got treated very differently," Darriel said.

Emmett smiled encouragingly. If Darriel felt he could talk, Emmett would listen.

"In my pack, only females were mates. Male omegas remained the property of the alpha."

Emmett squeezed his hand lightly. "Chrissy told me a little. You know Ryker's not like that, right?"

The fearful look Darriel shot him told Emmett his guess had been spot-on. Darriel gazed at Emmett as if he desperately wanted to believe him but wasn't sure.

"I know talk is cheap, and you can only really know that for sure by getting to know us, but I promise this is a good pack." He hesitated. "Can I ask you something?"

"Of course," Darriel said shyly.

"We still have a child—Calvin; he's about seven, we think—from one of the omega houses. There are a few omegas still missing, but we're trying to find his family. He says he doesn't ever remember an omega, but I'm asking everyone from Mills River just in case."

Darriel shook his head. "I've never heard the name, but I'm not surprised. The alpha had dozens of kids over the years, all growing up to be his personal army. The oldest are in their twenties."

"That's..." Emmett couldn't even think of a word. He sighed. "I know this sounds awful and selfish, but half of me is hoping he never turns up."

BABY AND THE WOLF

Emmett's hand flew to his mouth. It sounded a million times worse now that he'd said it out loud.

"It's easy to get attached."

"Understatement," Emmett agreed helplessly.

"I could imagine them having huge problems with the kids that don't belong to anyone."

Emmett blanched. "*Kids?*"

Darriel nodded. "You mentioned a Calvin, but I can name another six or seven off the top of my head."

"Is there any way their omegas were in other houses?"

"If the pups were over ten, yes. That was when they started their training."

"You sound like you were there a long time."

For a second, Darriel looked defeated, and then he buried his head in his hands briefly, and simply nodded.

"We haven't been able to find any more children."

"I doubt you will," Darriel said but wouldn't look him in the eye

"He had a lot of land though. They're searching." Ryker said the new alpha was doing his best.

"You might want to dig out back beyond the pig sheds."

A chill ran all the way down Emmett's spine. "What?"

"The kids who never shifted and weren't omegas. The enforcers would just turn up and drag them out. We never saw them again."

Emmett felt every drop of blood drain from his face.

"Riggs used to joke he'd feed me to the pigs if I lost another one."

Emmett didn't know which to react to first. No, he did. Ryker could have the first part of that sentence because Emmett couldn't even bear to think about it. "You've lost a baby?"

Darriel let out a sharp breath. "Four."

"I'm so sorry."

"Riggs didn't seem to understand that using me as a punching bag when I was pregnant wasn't a good idea, but the last time I lost this one all on my own. Riggs was furious because it was his."

"I thought—"

"That the enforcers were only allowed to touch us once we were already pregnant with the alpha's child?"

Emmett nodded. Not that it made it any better.

"Normally, the only way to bring on an omega's first heat is by their mate or their alpha. Sometimes very fertile omegas will have pre-heats, but they wouldn't go into one properly until then. I was compelled to come into heat the first time at fifteen, which is very painful. Then it was a regular occurrence every other month.. Pack wolves, but omegas especially, are pretty much screwed if their alpha commands them to do something." Emmett didn't like this. It was rape, pure and simple. "Couple that with being given something to drink to 'loosen us up,' and the alpha gets a very horny, very willing hole whenever he wants one."

Emmett shook his head. Barbaric was the wrong word—this was monstrous. "How old are you?"

"Twenty-one," Darriel said. "And I've been in this nightmare since my father died in a challenge."

"Shit," Emmett said with feeling, and Darriel smiled.

"My mom brought me to the pack after my father was killed. He was an enforcer for the losing alpha, and after he was defeated, all the enforcers were slaughtered. She knew I was an omega, but she believed the story he was pushing about the pack being a welcoming place for omegas." Darriel hesitated. "I'm not sure what you know about omega wolf history, but the birth rate has taken a dive and omegas are sought after."

Emmett nodded. "Chrissy told me."

"There are still a lot of packs disbanding because there aren't enough wolves to keep them going, but as soon as he found out I was an omega, I was taken into one of the houses, and I never saw my mom again."

Emmett blinked back tears. That was too close to home. "I'm sure Ryker could contact the new alpha for you."

Darriel shook his head. "She's dead. I found out she died about three years ago." Darriel's first sob seemed to almost take him by surprise, and he covered his face with his hands, trying to stop them. Emmett desperately wanted to hold him, but he didn't want to hurt his ribs. In the end, he just got on the bed and lay next to him and let him cry. Darriel moved so they were touching, and Emmett held his hand.

Darriel cried himself out. Sometime later, after Emmett was sure he was asleep, he got off the bed. He left the chips, fruit, and juice, then walked back to the kitchen with the sandwiches. He wasn't especially hungry anymore.

CHAPTER TWELVE

EMMETT WAS SITTING on the steps when Ryker found him. Ryker sat behind him and pulled Emmett onto his lap. Emmett turned into him without saying a word. They just sat for a minute and watched the kids. Ryker knew he'd talked to Darriel. Emmett didn't need to spell it out, but he needed to tell him and haltingly repeated what Darriel had said.

"He's safe now, and I will pass on what he said." Ryker glanced at the kids. "Why are you sitting here?"

Emmett waved to where the kids were pretending to be lion shifters and roaring at each other. "Sarah seemed to think one of them should be the king of the jungle and boss the others about, so to save an argument, I said I was the king." He sighed. "Of course, that meant I had to sit on a throne, and these steps are hard."

Ryker slid his hand underneath Emmett and rubbed gently. Emmett groaned. "You can't do that."

"Why?" Ryker said innocently but had to stop when he was spotted by Calvin, who ran up the steps to greet him. Emmett smiled. It wasn't just him who couldn't get enough of the alpha. Calvin was equally besotted.

"It's normal," Ryker said when Calvin had been persuaded to go back

VICTORIA SUE

and play. His face flushed a little. "When pups haven't had a lot of security, I mean. They latch onto either the alpha or someone similar."

Emmett nodded. Of course, it could have something to do with the fact that no matter how busy Ryker was, he always found time for Calvin. He usually woke up to them either outside playing or Calvin eating an early breakfast while Ryker tackled the paperwork that seemed to be piling up.

"Any news?" Emmett asked quietly. He knew the scouts had returned with reports on the missing omegas. His dad had come back with them but had disappeared inside. Emmett loved that he was visiting more and more, and he was planning on asking him to stay and eat supper with them. Zeke had also taken an interest in how Darriel was doing and often asked Emmett if he could help with anything.

Ryker shook his head. "We doubt at this point they'll ever be found. There's a chance the shifted wolves have either gone feral—"

"*What?*" Emmett whispered.

"If they've remained shifted for a long time. They can remain wild so long, it's easy to forget their human side." He shrugged. "Although we're not really talking long enough for that to happen. It's just a good way of hiding out from everyone at the moment."

"And the non-shifters?" He knew they were most worried because Riggs hadn't been found and there might be another cave full of omegas similar to the one they had found Calvin in.

"Not so far. The problem is, we're talking hundreds of miles, thousands if he has access to a vehicle. And because of the pack problems with population, everyone is so mistrustful. I wouldn't even be allowed on pack property in a lot of cases. Then, if I started asking about missing omegas, I'd be lucky if I was just thrown out."

"You see," Emmett said. "That's what I don't get. How come that beta got away with shooting you? I mean, why weren't the cops involved?"

"Packs police themselves. No one would involve the humans or they would end up with bigger problems. Not forgetting," Ryker added, "because of what we do, you're only seeing the worst shifters. There are a lot of good and honorable shifters. A lot of packs are like family."

Emmett raised his head for a kiss. "Like this one?"

BABY AND THE WOLF

Ryker obliged, and they were silent for a full minute. "Not that I don't love a kiss, but I came to find you for something else actually."

Emmett laid his head back on Ryker's shoulder and watched the kids. "So long as you don't need me for any more rescue missions, I'm good."

Ryker chuckled. "It's about Kai."

"What?" Emmett asked, immediately interested.

"I've been approached by an Alpha Kendrick from Mississippi. He's taken over a small pack since his father died, and he's wanting to expand. He's very short of wolves, and he's asking if we have any omegas interested in moving there."

"Would it be safe?"

"I don't know the pack, but the request comes through the shifter council, which means the pack has to be regulated. I've already mentioned it to Jason, and I was going to ask Kai. I wondered if you wanted to be there."

Definitely. If he could help Kai, he would. They walked into Kai's room, and Kai listened attentively while Ryker explained. He didn't react, neither pleasure nor fear, and Emmett was confused. "You don't have to go anywhere," Emmett said after it didn't look like Kai was going to reply.

Kai looked down at the floor, then at Ryker. "You've been good to me, Alpha, but I have to start my life at some point."

"And that can't be here?" Emmett asked softly.

"I hoped it could, but—" He shrugged.

"But you have friends. Ryker's going to get the pack ratified."

"I know," Kai said and smiled ruefully. He looked at Emmett and hesitated. Ryker took the hint and said he'd wait outside. Emmett walked up to Kai and hugged him.

"I would miss you so much."

Kai looked up at him and smiled determinedly. "I have to do it right this time."

Emmett wanted to ask "right for whom," but that wouldn't have been fair, so he let it go.

Practically the moment they left Kai, Marco found them and said he wanted to do Emmett's first scan. Emmett was thrilled. He hadn't asked Marco because between Kai getting close to his due date and Darriel needing a lot of help, plus the other omegas and kids who had arrived, Marco had been rushed off his feet, and no matter how much Emmett liked Dinah, there was no way he was going to discuss pregnancy and childbirth with her. Kai had told him some basics, which quite frankly had scared Emmett to death, but he could hardly say that to Kai when Kai was going to have his pup soon.

They went into the room Marco had set up as his temporary clinic. Emmett let Ryker help him onto the bed. Ryker had been amazing since the cave rescue. His schedule was full of things to get the pack arranged, but he made time to check on Emmett and usually Calvin at least every couple of hours when they weren't together.

Marco started unpacking a small case that looked like it contained a laptop. Ryker nodded toward it. "Is that the new tech everyone was excited about?"

Emmett glanced at Marco, then back at the computer. "What is it?"

"A portable ultrasound machine," he said proudly. "Zeke has bought two of them. One for the ranger's station and one for here."

"Very nice," Emmett murmured, still not seeing what was so amazing. All pregnant humans were offered ultrasounds, so wasn't this the norm?

"Shifters tend not to need any sort of medical intervention to give birth. Most packs don't even have a medically trained midwife, some not even a pack mother who has experience," Marco commented and started attaching leads. "Now, I'm going to warn you. There's not going to be much to see at this stage, even though you have a visible bump. Shifter bodies prepare differently. The little guy will still be tiny, so we're just checking heart rate and confirming a delivery date." Marco fiddled with some switches, and the sound of a heartbeat filled the room.

"Oh my," Emmett said in awe. Ryker bent down to kiss him on the forehead.

"Listen to him go."

"Him?" Emmett teased.

Ryker shrugged. "I don't care so long as they are healthy."

"Do you understand that male omegas generally have smaller babies because of the lack of room?" Marco asked.

BABY AND THE WOLF

"They do?" Emmett said. "I mean yes. I know we're not pregnant for as long a time as human women."

Marco nodded but kept his eyes on the screen. "Shifters give birth not long after human babies would be considered fully formed. It's only their shifter genes that makes the babies breathe on their own. Male omegas are born with a much smaller uterus. It expands in the same way a female's does but having the internal organs of both sexes leaves little space."

"Kai told me that he'd run out of room," Emmett said to Ryker. "When I asked why he wasn't eating, just drinking milkshakes."

"Exactly," Marco agreed. "Because the abdominal cavity is squashed as the baby grows, there is little room for food. There is also a direct link enabling osmosis."

Emmett's eyebrows raised. "What?"

Marco grinned. "How do you think you actually get pregnant?"

Emmett blinked slowly. He hadn't, to be honest. He was so stunned at actually finding out he was pregnant, the mechanics of it had never occurred to him.

"I can explain when and if you want to know. It's fascinating, really, but the problem male omegas have is that their babies are born early. Shifter babies are usually pretty hardy, so most of the time it isn't an issue, but there's a very small time frame between the baby being able to breathe on its own and delivery. If a human baby was born at twenty weeks, it would have serious problems and would be unlikely to survive. Luckily, shifters are much different. Their lungs and other internal organs are developed. Everything is just smaller."

Marco took a few more measurements, but Emmett could tell with his relaxed posture he wasn't worried. "There you go," Marco said. He turned off the machine and went to wipe the gel off of Emmett before thinking better of it and handing the tissues to Ryker. Emmett basked in the care and attention Ryker showed. Then Ryker helped him sit up.

"Can you tell me what actually happens? I mean, I've seen women give birth on TV, but—" He looked down at himself, feeling his skin heat.

"You have a longer anogenital distance than other males. Not so much

VICTORIA SUE

to be hugely different, and not that you will even have thought about it. It can sometimes even occur naturally in human males."

Emmett felt a little stupid until he saw the same expression on Ryker's face. "I have a what?"

Marco grinned and rolled his eyes. "Sorry. I've been taking a class all week, and I'm still in medical-speak mode. Your anogenital distance is basically the gap between your scrotum and your anus. You won't have even noticed, but distance-wise, it gives you an extra inch."

"I'm pretty sure I'm gonna need more than an inch to get a baby out of me." Emmett could feel his face heat even more. No wonder Ryker hadn't wanted to tell him.

"You have a very small membrane behind your scrotum that thins and opens during labor in exactly the same way a woman's cervix expands."

Emmett shuddered. All of a sudden, he wasn't sure he wanted to know. "Yeah?" he said weakly and swallowed.

"What the main thing to concentrate on is that this method of birth—while secret from the human world—has been the norm for centuries."

Emmett took in the steady gray eyes and relaxed. "Okay." He decided to concentrate on what else he wanted to know. "I wanted to ask about my passing out." Ryker looked likewise relieved to have the subject changed.

Marco gave him all of his attention while Emmett explained. "There are a few tests we can run," Marco said. "Simple ones like an echocardiogram or a tilt table test to check and see if your blood pressure dips. I'd want to do a little more research, though, as I don't have experience with this." He nodded to himself. "But from what you've told me, I think your problem may be resolved with diet. Panther omegas especially, more so than wolves or bears, need a high protein content in their diet. The cave-in was a scary time, and you suffered no dizziness or nausea, did you?"

Emmett shook his head. "To be honest, I've never felt better."

Marco grinned. "There's also the fact that your blood volume just increased by fifty percent."

"It did?" Emmett said. "Why?"

"Pregnancy side effect." He glanced at Ryker as he offered instructions. "Small meals and often. Dense in nutrients and high in protein. There's

BABY AND THE WOLF

nothing regarding panther shifters that's different. I honestly think that diet will completely address this."

Emmett blew out a breath of relief. "I was always hungry. Not so much when I was little but definitely after I lived with Barry." And Barry had made him feel greedy and selfish. "It was easier to get used to eating less." A thought occurred to him. "Why would he keep me hungry when he knew what I was?"

Ryker scowled. "It was deliberate. To keep you weak and controlled. If you'd have been healthy, you might have been more difficult to keep hidden."

Ryker clasped his hand. Emmett met his eyes and saw the promise in them, the care and affection. Not only that Emmett wouldn't go hungry, but more importantly that he wouldn't feel stupid for feeling so. That he was finally normal. Emmett nodded. He tried to forget about his uncle, but he didn't think they'd seen the last of him.

"It's not the amount that even matters here, more the nutritional value," Marco carried on.

"What do you know of the local panther clan?" Ryker asked when Marco had finished.

Marco didn't answer for a moment, then sighed. "Not much. I escaped mine. And sorry, Alpha, but I am unwilling to say from where."

Ryker shrugged. "That's not necessary. I want to know if what Emmett's uncle told him about panther omegas is true."

"You are certainly very rare, and should you wish, without a direct female available you could take over the clan, but it wouldn't be easy. There may be challenges if you have, say, female cousins or nieces. But panthers are civilized. We're talking a simple vote."

"He seemed to think it would make him a lot of money," Emmett added.

Marco huffed. "He wouldn't be joking. Panther clans are usually worth millions."

Emmett's eyebrows raised. "I thought he was exaggerating."

He nodded and looked at Ryker. "Where do you get your funds from?"

"Discounting Zeke?" Ryker asked ruefully. "People who live here who can pay a minimal contribution. We own a large group of vacation cabins over in Sapphire that we rent to humans. Investments."

"Which is typical pack dynamics, but clans don't live in a community; they all live externally. They still do, however, contribute up to twenty percent of their income on a sliding scale to the Panthera. She's very wealthy."

"But what does she actually do?" Emmett asked.

"Makes more money. There is an emergency fund, and then there's the claw, of course. All panthers, once named to the clan, are given an amount of money, a generous startup if you like, plus a house. They are expected to make more and contribute to the clan, but it comes with certain lifestyle rules I wasn't happy with."

"What's a claw?" Emmett asked, not sure if he wasn't being teased.

Ryker put his hand on his heart. "Google it by all means, but a group of panthers is called a claw."

"Correct," Marco agreed. "Except panther shifters call it a clan. We use the term claw to refer to the equivalent of a wolf pack's enforcers."

"Scary guys," Ryker murmured.

Marco paused as if he was struggling with something but just nodded. "They're not a group you want to meet." He hesitated. "I caution you not to trust your uncle."

He didn't need that caution. "So, not only would Barry get rich, he would have his own personal army?" Emmett shivered.

"I understand you're friends with Darriel?"

Emmett accepted the change of subject, knowing Marco didn't want to discuss any more. "I only met him less than a week ago, but I hope so. Why?"

"He might appreciate someone with him while he has his scan. He's nervous."

"He's having a scan?" Emmett asked in surprise. "*He's pregnant?*"

"He's bleeding, and today was the first time he admitted it to me. He says he lost the baby, but he's still spotting."

Emmett frowned. He remembered that, but then that made no sense

BABY AND THE WOLF

with what he'd just been told. "How—" He stopped awkwardly as both Ryker and Marco looked at him, but then Marco's face cleared.

"It *should* open during labor. If it opens early, there's bleeding. If it opens too much, there's a large chance of miscarriage."

Emmett closed his eyes briefly. Hadn't Darriel gone through enough? "Do you think there's a chance?"

Marco sighed. "I doubt he's still pregnant. I would just like to see if this is unhealed damage. I've tried before to get him to let me do a scan, but this is the first time he's agreed. He won't let any alpha near enough to him to see if they could get a heartbeat." And Emmett couldn't do that. Ryker bent to kiss him and promised to keep an eye on Calvin while Emmett was busy, and they went to see Darriel.

And Emmett got the shock of his life when they walked in. "*Dad?*" His dad was sitting in the corner chair, and he put down the book he held as they came in. As he stood, he glanced at Darriel and smiled gently. "We can finish it later. I'm hanging around for a bit." He closed the door quietly as he left.

Darriel smiled but seemed uncomfortable, so Emmett didn't say anything else. Marco had an incredibly gentle manner about him, and Emmett checked, but Darriel definitely wanted him to stay. Darriel's eyes rounded as Marco unpacked the case and explained what he was doing. "I've had four pregnancies and never had an ultrasound."

Emmett looked up at him but wasn't sure why he was surprised with what he had learned. "You haven't?"

Darriel shook his head. "Most of the time we didn't even get a pack mother."

"Not always so unusual with some packs," Marco said mildly.

"You think my body didn't absorb everything?" Darriel whispered.

Marco stilled and met Emmett's gaze. Emmett understood Marco couldn't let Darriel get excited like he probably normally would. The chance of a baby surviving what had been done to Darriel was impossible.

"Just remember things are different and you're not on your own any longer," Emmett promised. Darriel nodded, seeming unable to speak, and Marco apologized before he gently lifted Darriel's top. Emmett was sitting in the chair on the other side and remained quiet but held on to Darriel's hand tightly.

"I've agreed to be based here permanently."

Emmett brightened and watched Darriel relax. They needed a medic here, and it might make everyone feel better. Darriel nodded, and Marco smiled again. Emmett helped get Darriel settled on his back, and Marco used gel.

"We've even got the stuff that's not too cold." He hummed in approval.

Darriel closed his eyes as if he couldn't bear to look as the screen flickered on.

Marco paused and stared at the screen, and then he turned a knob. A second later, the sound of a heartbeat was loud and fast. It seemed to be tripping over itself, and Darriel's eyes shot open.

"That's impossible."

Marco shrugged. "Obviously not," he replied and started clicking scans, seemingly taking measurements.

"I can't believe it," Darriel said in awe. "Can—I mean, do you know what it is?"

Emmett hoped he was the only one who heard the small pause before Marco answered.

"Which one?" Marco said carefully and pointed to the screen, and it took them both a minute.

"What do you mean?" Darriel said breathlessly. Although it was obvious to Emmett what he could see.

"What I mean," Marco said deliberately casually, "is that somehow two pups have survived." He pointed to both images.

"But that's impossible."

"It's rare, certainly," Marco acknowledged.

Darriel gasped. "What sexes are they?"

"Impossible to say at this stage. I'm guessing you're about six weeks pregnant, if that." Marco smiled, and Emmett glanced at Darriel.

"Really?" Darriel was smiling, but he didn't sound excited. His lip wobbled, and Emmett clasped his hand. "That sounds about right." He looked away and bit his lip, and Emmett's heart broke, understanding he was probably trying to forget how this had happened.

Marco clicked a few more buttons, then turned to Darriel. "How do you feel?" Emmett's pulse picked up. The question sounded casual, but Emmett didn't think it was.

Darriel's gaze seemed glued to the screen. "I got to three months once. The last time, the heart just stopped." His eyes filled again. "I never got to hear the heartbeat at all."

Marco nodded, unhooked the machine, and wiped the gel from Darriel. He helped him sit up and get comfortable before Emmett got a chance to, and then he sat down on the bed and looked at Darriel. He smiled gently. "I want you to stay on bed rest until I come back and do another scan. You can get up to pee, but—"

"But why?" Darriel interrupted. "You just saw them." He smiled. "I still can't believe it."

Marco hesitated, and Emmett's heart dropped to his boots. This time, Darriel picked up on it.

"What aren't you telling me?" He pulled his hand away from Emmett as if he had to protect himself.

"Both their heart rates are a little slow," Marco admitted, "and we need to keep an eye on it. Obviously, I'm really concerned about the bleeding."

"You mean they still might die?" Darriel whispered.

Marco didn't answer, but he didn't need to. "Take advantage of the rest while you can."

Darriel nodded and turned his face to the side. "I understand."

Marco glanced helplessly at Emmett. "If you come out with me, I will leave instructions for you and Dinah." Emmett took the hint and promised he would be back in a few minutes.

Darriel closed his eyes. "Actually, if you wouldn't mind, I'm kind of tired. Maybe this afternoon?" It was a polite dismissal that Emmett could do nothing about.

They both left. Emmett held the door open so Marco could get all of his equipment through. They walked to the kitchen. Zeke and Ryker were in there, and both of them looked up when they walked in. "What's wrong?" Ryker asked immediately when Emmett walked into his arms.

Marco briefed them both. "The slow heart rate combined with the bleeding makes his miscarriage risk much higher. Add that to his history and a multiple pregnancy, which is rare for male omegas, and he's got serious problems. I want to get back here as quickly as possible, but I still have a ten-day commitment to the ranger service to work through."

"No, you don't," Zeke said grimly. "I'll take care of it. I'll fly someone in every day if I have to. Darriel needs you here."

Emmett gazed at his dad in astonishment, but Marco just nodded, then turned his attention to Emmett. "Ryker is going to get a proper clinic here, but there's a huge difference between a clinic and a neonatal intensive care unit."

"I'm glad I had my scan first," Emmett said. He would have felt so guilty getting excited for his baby when Darriel was going through this. "That's why you did it this way around?" Emmett said in understanding.

"He has a difficult history. I was being cautious."

"Is there anything I can do?"

"Be his friend," Marco said simply and looked at Ryker. "Alpha, I will be back tonight after my shift, if that's okay?"

"That's a long day for you," Ryker pointed out.

"I'd be happier seeing Kai again as well." Marco's face softened.

Ryker gazed at Marco thoughtfully, then nodded. "I'll warn the scouts you'll be visiting late and make sure they know you have unlimited access."

Emmett thanked Marco and glanced up at Ryker.

Ryker put out his hand. "Got a minute?"

"I'll keep an eye on Calvin," Chrissy promised. He was sitting with two other kids at a table making cookies with Dinah. Emmett chuckled. He doubted Calvin had missed him, seeing as they seemed to be wearing more cookie dough than they were actually baking.

Emmett let Ryker lead him outside and around the back of the pack house. "I just wanted to check that you're okay."

Emmett stepped into Ryker's arms and laid his head on his chest. "We haven't had a minute, huh?" Having Calvin there wasn't really doing anything for their alone time.

"You seem to be taking a lot on."

Emmett squinted up at Ryker. Was that a criticism? A warning? "Too much?"

Ryker slid his hand under Emmett's chin and raised it. He took possession of his mouth in a long, lingering kiss that left Emmett wanting so much more. "You are amazing, do you know that? In the space of a month, you've found out you're a panther shifter and pregnant, taken part in rescuing a bunch of kids, *and* helping a kid who seems to have adopted you."

Emmett gazed into deep brown eyes. "Maybe I should ask you how you feel about it."

"Which part," hummed Ryker, blowing gently on Emmett's neck and raising goose bumps. "The part where I get to mate the sexiest panther shifter I've ever seen?" He nibbled on his chin. "Or the part where I get a family?"

Which was a lovely thought. Then Emmett remembered what Darriel had said about the pig pens and did his best not to cry.

CHAPTER THIRTEEN

RYKER WAS GETTING FED up with being woken by his phone, and he reached for it before it woke up Calvin and Emmett. He slipped out of the bedroom and answered it.

"I just heard from the alpha down in Mills River," Red said. "Apparently they have confirmed there have been no more sightings of Riggs on their land. He apologizes and has offered to help if you need him."

"I may have to pass this up to the shifter council. If he's still in the area, he might pose a threat to the human tourists. They would listen then."

"So I can leave it with you, Alpha?"

Ryker tried not to roll his eyes. He knew Red was half-serious, half ragging on him by giving him his new title. He hung up and went into the kitchen to brew coffee and put the kettle on for Emmett's tea. Emmett wanted to move back into the cabin, but Ryker couldn't risk it. He knew his gammas, especially with the new ones, had the area covered, so they were safe; it just wasn't a long-term solution. He even remembered Calvin's juice, and he looked critically around the large pack kitchen. Nope, it was no good. He wanted their own space. He just couldn't decide whether to build onto the pack house or to move into a new cabin. He liked the way his old one backed up to the forest and was hidden from the pack house, but maybe that wasn't a good look for the alpha with one definitely and maybe even two kids to think about. The thought of Calvin running in the wrong direction and getting lost filled him with horror.

While he was waiting, he called Zeke.

"Ryker? Everything okay with Emmett?" He heard the faint alarm in Zeke's voice and knew he had to remember Zeke was essentially a new father as well.

"Everything's good." He quickly told him about the phone call he'd just had, but as a human, this time there was nothing Zeke could do.

"Marco's replacement starts today. She's just going to need a day to orientate herself, and she should be good to go. How's Darriel?"

"Not so good. He's been bleeding." He heard Zeke swear softly on the other end of the line. "I appreciate you getting Marco here permanently."

"His replacement's really good. She might not even need him there today. She lives locally and is based near Sapphire."

He thanked Zeke, hung up, and carried in the peppermint tea, along with his coffee and Calvin's juice, and sat down on the bed, chuckling to himself. All he could see of Emmett was a mound of blankets. Calvin was likewise huddled up under a similar pile of blankets on the small cot in the far corner. They really should start thinking about getting him into his own room. He waved the tea in the air, hoping it might rouse the two sleepyheads, and after a moment, Emmett cracked open an eyelid.

He smiled and glanced over at Calvin. "I think he's got a lot of sleep to catch up on."

Ryker grinned and kept his voice low. "His senses are telling him he's safe though. He's a shifter, and no amount of whispering would help if he felt threatened. I made your tea."

Emmett nodded but didn't reach for it. He pressed a hand to his belly. "I feel—" He cut off and shot out of bed, nearly catching Ryker with his foot.

Ryker followed, placing both mugs on the dresser. He winced when he heard Emmett getting sick, then ran to the kitchen for some cool water and tissues. He jogged back and knocked on the bathroom door. When Emmett didn't respond, he let himself in.

Emmett flushed the toilet and sat down on the floor.

Ryker bent down. "What is it?"

"Either I ate something that doesn't agree with me, or every awful pregnancy tale is going to happen. It probably means I'm going to get stretch marks," Emmett wailed, shivering.

"You're cold." He pulled down a robe from the back of the door and draped it around Emmett's shoulders. "Let me help you back to bed."

"I can't," Emmett said pitifully. "I might get sick again, and Calvin's in there." Yep, they definitely needed more room. Emmett wouldn't be persuaded, so Ryker simply sat down next to him. After a few minutes, Emmett decided to brush his teeth but still didn't want to go back to bed. He was shivering, even in the robe.

"How about if we just sit down on the bed? Then it's easier for you to get to the bathroom if you need to?"

"Okay," Emmett agreed, and before Emmett could change his mind, Ryker simply picked him up and carried him back to the bedroom. Emmett turned his face into Ryker's chest and closed his eyes. Ryker sat down on the bed and dragged the blanket over them both, cradling him close. "I hate being sick."

Ryker dropped a kiss on Emmett's head. "If it is the pregnancy, we'll go ask Dinah about it when you feel okay. She'll have something to help."

Emmett nodded, and they just sat awhile.

"Any better?"

Emmett seemed to have to think. "I'm good here."

Which wasn't exactly the answer to Ryker's question, but then he smiled. If he was really, really lucky, maybe it was the answer he was hoping for. They hadn't talked about anything, other than his declaration just before Emmett crawled into the cave. He'd bitten Emmett. He didn't even know as a half shifter he could do that, but the scar was a permanent reminder they were mated. The pack meeting, Darriel arriving, and Calvin all seemed to have taken over things, but he knew they had to sit down and talk, and as soon as possible.

* * *

VICTORIA SUE

EMMETT LOOKED nervous when he padded out of the house later that morning. Ryker had managed to sneak Calvin out when he'd woken, gotten him a snack, and they were now sitting on the decking above the steps and he was trying to explain to him what it felt like to be a wolf. Calvin had shifter instincts. His hearing, sight, and health were stronger, even if Sarah was right and he was an omega and wouldn't shift. And it wasn't that they doubted Sarah. It was that it didn't matter. Alpha, omega, *space alien*. Calvin had wormed his way into both of their hearts. The only thing Ryker could tell him with any certainty was that at least one of his parents was a wolf.

Although he supposed now that they had the ultrasound machine, they could see what he looked like inside. Or could they? Was it something they were born with or developed? He had no clue.

Emmett, wrapped in Ryker's mom's blanket, came and sat in the rocking chair on the deck. Ryker sat with his back to the pack house wall, knees bent, and Calvin had tucked himself between them, his back to Ryker's chest. Calvin beamed when Emmett sat down, but Ryker guessed he was comfy because he made no move to leave the shelter provided by Ryker's knees.

"What if I'm not a proper wolf though?" Calvin chewed his lip. It was clear this had been bothering the little scrap for a while, not exactly surprising when he saw how the old alpha had treated his omegas. Emmett sent Ryker a worried look, but he had this.

"What do you think a proper wolf is?"

Calvin tilted his head as if he was having to think hard. "You," he said at last. "You're the alpha."

Ryker bent and kissed the top of his head. "But I'm a mixed breed."

Calvin screwed his face up. "But you're the alpha."

"Exactly. I can shift, yes, but my mom was a human. She wasn't even an omega."

Calvin turned to stare at Ryker in shock. "And they let you be the alpha?"

Emmett chuckled.

"Nobody *let* me do anything," Ryker said, smiling. "The wolves here, the ones who helped Emmett rescue you?" Calvin nodded. "They all voted and decided to make me alpha because I was doing the job anyway." Calvin still looked stunned, but Ryker decided to press his advantage home. "The important thing is that no one can say you can't be something." He tapped Calvin's chest. "If you have the heart of a shifter, you can be whatever you choose. You could be the alpha one day."

Calvin gaped. "I could?"

"But you have to work hard. You'll be starting school soon, huh?"

Calvin didn't look impressed. "Riggs said book learning was for those that were too dumb to be a proper wolf." It was obviously word for word one of the lessons Riggs had rammed down his throat.

"You know that's not true though," Emmett said.

Calvin glanced at Emmett. "Did you go to school?"

Emmett nodded. "I loved school. We got to play and make cool stuff like rocket ships."

"A rocket ship?" Calvin asked in awe.

Ryker laughed, picked Calvin up as he stood, and set him down gently next to Emmett's chair. "I have an important job for you," Ryker said. "And only gamma cadets can do this."

Calvin's eyes rounded. "What's a gamma cadet?"

"It's what you call special shifters that when they grow a bit bigger will be in the gamma squad and help the alpha."

"Can I be in the gamma squad?" Calvin asked eagerly.

Ryker swallowed down the sudden lump in his throat. "Yep, but that means you get to do important jobs for me."

Calvin nodded so violently Ryker expected his head to fall off. "What do I do?"

"Well, for starters, we need to make sure Emmett gets looked after while I make pancakes. Can you do that?" Calvin looked awed and doubtful at the same time. "If you come in with me, we're going to get him a glass of juice, and without spilling any, you need to carefully bring it back out and stay with him to make sure he drinks it. That'll earn you at least two points for my new gamma cadet board. You need at least five points every day to make the team."

Calvin immediately clasped the hand Ryker offered, and they went inside to start gamma cadet training.

Emmett was led into the kitchen by Calvin after he'd drunk all his juice and was encouraged to sit down again. Emmett thanked Calvin solemnly and announced if he kept it up, he had no doubt he would make an excellent gamma cadet.

Ryker popped another pancake into the oven to keep warm. "Why don't you draw me a picture of a rocket? Then I have a surprise for you both after."

"I'm starving," Emmett said. Being sick earlier certainly wasn't bothering him now, and he asked Calvin to get some napkins while he put everything on the table. They ate comfortably, and then they walked back to their rooms. Calvin went to brush his teeth.

"I'm thinking we need a bigger place," Ryker said carefully.

Emmett looked around the room, then back at Ryker. "Another bedroom, certainly."

Ryker's heart picked up. "You, I mean, well—" *Ughh*. Ryker started again. "I meant what I said at the cave. About you being here, that is. I bit you." He looked up and met Emmett's eyes. "I'm not good at flowery words." Emmett looked up at him expectantly, and because he was too far away, he leaned over and plucked Emmett from his chair and sat him on his knee. He'd lost count of the number of times he'd done that, but if he was unsure about everything else, touch, closeness was what they both needed. He took in a deep breath. That was better. Emmett raised his hand and brushed an errant hair from Ryker's face. His hair was getting too long. He normally just hacked at it, but he'd been a bit distracted.

"I love being here," Emmett said. "I know this is sudden, and scary, but we have to think about the baby. I think this is the best place for them both." Ryker nodded eagerly. "And I'd like to help you with the pack."

Ryker agreed in case Emmett thought he wouldn't. "The alpha-mate has an important role."

Emmett smiled. "Is that what I am?"

"God, I hope so," Ryker admitted before he leaned down and kissed him. He tasted of sugar and syrup. Ryker's hand fell to Emmett's belly and

BABY AND THE WOLF

the definite mound there and rubbed it lovingly. He wasn't sure if Emmett had noticed it had grown. He guessed when Emmett broke off and looked down, he hadn't.

"Wow."

Ryker kissed him again. Emmett was rapidly becoming the most important thing in his life. He glanced to the bathroom and heard Calvin still brushing his teeth.

"We're going to need to make a decision soon." Although he had a feeling it had already been made.

Emmett followed his gaze and nodded his understanding. "I think we both made it."

Which Ryker thought Emmett deserved a kiss for and thoroughly showed his approval.

Calvin bounced back in with his T-shirt on inside out, and Emmett smiled sweetly and reached over for him. Calvin eyed them both, probably wondering what Emmett was doing on Ryker's knee, but Ryker recognized a little longing in the expression. Shifters—he knew—were very touch oriented. They got comfort from close ties with their pack. He reached out, and in another second, Calvin was snuggled in as well.

Emmett kissed his cheek. "It's a good thing you have room."

Plenty, thought Ryker. Room on his lap and room in his heart.

CHAPTER FOURTEEN

RYKER DIDN'T SEEM to have a minute to breathe in the next two weeks either. He was getting his pack together slowly, but it seemed like every time he thought they had gotten something organized, another problem reared its head.

And the latest was driving him crazy. There had been three odd incidents. A burst pipe, which could be blamed on the icy winter that had suddenly done an about-face to summer without pausing for spring in between and had flooded the kitchen.

The second had been one of their trucks catching fire. That had freaked him out because Chrissy had started the engine and then remembered she had forgotten her drill. If she hadn't gotten back out, it would have caught fire with her in it. The trouble was the fire had ruined any chance of Ryker getting a scent, and it hadn't occurred to him to check the pipe.

Both of those could have been explained away. The fire had damaged everything, so they couldn't know for sure, but his gut told him something was wrong. They had identified at least three different strange scents recently, but none of them had returned, so it could easily be wild wolves this close to the national park. Zeke had offered video surveillance, but Ryker had nixed that idea. He wanted a pack, not a prison.

The third incident had involved Calvin. He was playing with his two best buddies from the cave, Joshua and Mira, and they had wandered a little too close to the tree line. Mira at five had never shifted, and Damien, their omega, had been distracted when Joshua tripped and scraped his knee. Joshua was four and a scraped knee meant the world was ending. Just as he finished dealing with that, Mira had come running up to Damien, saying a man was talking to Calvin.

Damien shouted for Chrissy, who was the closest, and she had run out immediately. She had gotten to a truck just as the driver gunned it, leaving Calvin there. Deciding to make sure Calvin was unharmed, the driver got away. Everyone had come running, and Ryker, Fox, Red, and Chrissy had all shifted, but the truck must have headed straight for the main highway, and they had no chance tracking it.

All Calvin could tell them was it definitely hadn't been a wolf. He never got out of the car, just mentioned he'd lost a dog and asked questions about who Calvin lived with. He'd seemed nice and was happy to hear he lived with the new alpha and his omega.

Ryker had met Emmett's worried gaze. "That's it. We're staying in the pack house full-time."

The local sheriff patrolled, but all they had was a vague description and a black truck. Chrissy hadn't seen the man or a license plate. Calvin hadn't been frightened, and if the man hadn't panicked and gone when he'd seen an adult, they would have just bought his story about losing a dog. There was an explanation for every incident, but Ryker had an uneasy feeling about the whole thing. He'd increased the patrols as much as he could.

They were sitting down this afternoon to go through the list of more new applications for the pack. Darriel was still on bed rest, and Emmett was visiting him and Kai every day. What surprised Ryker was that of all people, so was Zeke, or as much as he could. They'd both watched him arrive with another half dozen books. He'd smiled and just said Darriel was interested in Philip Pullman.

Emmett watched him go inside. "Who's Philip Pullman?"

Ryker had no idea. "Are you coming to the meeting about the pack?"

Emmett nodded. "I'll just go check on Kai, then I'll be right in."

Ryker slid an arm around him before he could move away. "How are you feeling?"

Emmett nuzzled his neck, and Ryker chuckled. "Me too, but I didn't mean that." Emmett had stopped being sick. He'd changed his teas to regular black with a plain cracker first thing, and it seemed to be working.

Ryker nodded and drew Emmett in closer. He didn't have a recognizable shifter scent. That hadn't changed, but he had an Emmett scent and Ryker couldn't get enough of it. He tilted Emmett's chin up and captured his lips. Emmett sagged against him, and Ryker loved that Emmett felt secure in the knowledge Ryker could support him. "Don't overdo things. How's Kai?"

"He was asleep when I called in earlier. But I'm really worried. I wish he'd stay and have the pup here."

Ryker nodded. The alpha from Mississippi had checked out and wanted Kai to move as soon as possible, preferably before he gave birth so that he had a couple of weeks to settle in. None of them wanted him to go, but Kai was being very stubborn. "Are you coming to meet my new betas?"

Emmett nodded. "I'm going to take Dinah's brownies. Have one more go at changing his mind."

Ryker approved of the brownie plan. "How many did she make?"

Emmett kissed him. "I'm sure I can find some spare."

HE HAD a meeting with Fox and Red. In any other circumstances they could both be alphas of their own pack. He doubted Red was interested, but Fox had a quiet strength about him that was appealing to the more vulnerable shifters. He needed to establish more betas or enforcers, and he was open to advice. He also wanted to see what they thought of the eleven extra pack applications. He walked into the small room off the kitchen he was thinking of using as a meeting room. He'd never needed one before. He just picked up the phone or went and found someone, but he had a feeling things would need better organizing now.

Chrissy walked in a moment later, followed by Emmett. Red was already seated. He grinned as Ryker walked in. "Should we like stand or something?"

Ryker stared him down. The joking had gotten out of hand. It was one thing between friends, but he didn't want any of the new members picking up on it. Red nodded once as if he understood and accepted the unspoken order. Chrissy put a piece of paper in front of them all. "These are the applications we've had since last week. We can—"

Fox came in. "Alpha, we've just had a call from the gate scouts." Ryker looked up and saw in Fox's face that he wasn't going to like what he was about to say. "Apparently the Panthera is down there with three of her clan, demanding to see Emmett. His uncle is with her."

Ryker immediately reached out for Emmett, and Emmett stood and walked into Ryker's outstretched arms. "She has no power over you," Ryker promised.

Fox looked at Ryker expectantly. "We can pull the scouts off for protection if we need to, but there are already nine of us."

"Ten," Dinah said defiantly, bustling in.

"Is Marco here?" Ryker asked.

"I think he's with Kai," Chrissy said.

"Go and warn him to stay away."

Emmett shot him a grateful glance. "I don't understand how she knows. My uncle wouldn't have told her."

"It doesn't matter," Ryker said. "Keep all the scouts in place and warn them. I don't trust this not to be another diversion." What if the man who had been talking to Calvin had been a panther? It made sense. Calvin would have assumed he was a human if he didn't smell wolf.

Twenty minutes later, they were standing on the steps to the pack house. Marco and Dinah had taken all the omegas and pups to the large room they were staying in. Zeke had immediately stood when Emmett had gone into Darriel's room and told him they were on their way, but Emmett had begged him to stay with Darriel. Ryker was stunned that Zeke had agreed. Emmett clasped Ryker's hand as the luxury SUV rolled into the clearing in front of the pack house. He wasn't surprised it was driven by a cat. The BMW's powerful engine certainly purred like one.

The man who got out surprised him. He was tall but not muscular. As he respectfully opened the door, his eyes weren't on the woman getting out, they were scanning every detail of the surrounding area. *A professional.*

Ryker heard the short inhale as Emmett saw his grandmother and realized from the photograph that Emmett's mom was the absolute double of her. A lot younger, but there was no doubt whose daughter she had been. And as she stared at Emmett—completely riveted—he realized her eyes were exactly the same shade of turquoise blue. This was going to be hard.

He gazed at the Panthera. She screamed money, but she also seemed classy. Like she didn't have to prove anything. He let go of Emmett's hand and jogged down the steps. "Panthera, you honor us." He could be respectful, right? She didn't reply. All her attention was on Emmett.

She took the steps she needed to get to Emmett. He stood, frozen. "You are so like your mother," she whispered.

His blue eyes darkened. "The one you had murdered?" he asked woodenly, then turned and walked inside.

EMMETT DIDN'T WAIT to see the effect his question had on her. He didn't care. He was struggling between fury and wanting to cry. Ryker caught up to him in seconds and clasped his hand, but Emmett didn't need a bodyguard for this. In fact, he knew for his own self-respect this was a battle he had to fight for himself. He squeezed Ryker's hand, but then let go and turned to see them follow him into the meeting room. Ryker didn't attempt to retake his hand, just maintained a solid presence next to him.

The Panthera walked into the room flanked by her men. A third came in next to Barry, who looked sulky. He'd seen that look on his uncle's face so many times, and it was usually followed by cruelty.

Never being good enough. Never doing things right. Not strong enough. Too weak. Too pathetic.

VICTORIA SUE

Emmett wondered briefly what had happened, then dismissed it. He wanted them gone, and as soon as she found out he wasn't interested in the clan, she would leave him alone.

One of the men next to her drew out a chair, and she sat and glanced up at Emmett. "Please sit down. I only want to talk."

Emmett could refuse, but as he looked at her for another moment, he capitulated. "What do you want?" And he sat.

"The first thing you should know is that I loved my daughter and would never harm her. The second is I only found out about you yesterday." She shot a look at Barry, and he swallowed.

"Yeah? Then why did she leave?"

"Josephine never liked clan politics, and she never wanted to be Panthera. It's my fault she ran. I pressured her into responsibility and didn't recognize that she was truly unhappy. Whatever you've been told about panther clans is probably true, but it is a fine line between wanting to bring about change and acting in the clan's best interests. I have made an awful lot of mistakes, but I would never hurt Josephine, and I would definitely never hurt you. It is, however, my fault she never believed that."

She glanced down but not before he saw her overbright eyes. She didn't answer for a moment, but then she visibly squared her shoulders and looked over at him.

"And because of that, she left. I heard reports later that she was seeing a human, and I tracked her down to the apartment she was living in."

"So you went to frighten her?" The bitter words were out before he could stop them, and he registered the pain that twisted her lips as they hit. He should have felt some sort of satisfaction, but he was just too hollowed out.

"I never saw her," she admitted. "A Panthera can tell immediately if a panther is pregnant, in a similar way to your wolves being able to hear a heartbeat, but as I didn't go—*couldn't* go—I never knew."

"Couldn't?" Emmett pounced on the word. He might not want this conversation, but it seemed he couldn't help himself.

"If I had gone to see her myself, it would have been a formal acknowledgment to the clan. They would have expected excommunication at the

BABY AND THE WOLF

very least, and as Panthera, I am as trapped by the rules as much as I have to enforce them." She swallowed. "So I sent Barry to go talk to her. To make sure she had money. That she was safe." She stared dispassionately at her son. "A mistake."

Emmett glanced at his uncle in shock. Not that he was surprised at the lie Barry had told him, and he knew it was a lie. He didn't know how or why...no, of course he did. Barry wanted the clan. He'd always wanted it. A sick feeling washed over Emmett as he stared at Barry. *How much had he wanted it?*

"Did you kill her?"

Barry blustered. "Of course not. She was my sister, and I loved her."

Another lie. A deep conviction settled over Emmett. "But you wanted the clan. When you found out about me, you knew what I was. I could get you the clan. She was in the way of you getting that."

The Panthera whipped her head around to Barry. "Is that true?"

He shook his head. "I was with you when Josie was killed. You know that."

She turned back to Emmett. "That is true. We found out from the police report when she had been killed."

"From the same witnesses that mysteriously disappeared as soon as the case was closed?" Emmett taunted and stood. "If that's true, why didn't you tell me what I was?" But he didn't wait for a reply—he knew. "Get out."

He scowled. "I kept you safe for years, and this is how you repay me?"

"Safe?" Emmett snapped incredulously. "You used me like some unpaid servant. You made me ill. Deliberately fed me a diet that would keep me sick. You lied to me. You even had one of the deputies in your pocket. You wanted the clan. Still want the clan, but your so-called beloved sister was in the way of that. How much did it cost you to get rid of her?"

Ryker stood. "Emmett, *no*."

"Or did you think it was money well spent?" Emmett railed, ignoring Ryker and Chrissy as they both tried to silence him. Well, no longer. He'd been silent for long enough. He might not be able to prove Barry had killed his mom, but he didn't have to listen to him or see him ever again.

Barry stood. A cruel smile seemed to hover on his lips, and Emmett wondered why he looked inexplicably pleased. Didn't he think Emmett meant it?

"You have insulted me in front of the Panthera," he said very slowly.

"And I'm supposed to give a rat's ass?"

Ryker tugged on his arm. "Emmett," he said warningly, but Emmett didn't care. He had no intention of making nice to these people.

"And as such," Barry continued calmly, "I demand the right to retribution."

Every wolf jumped to their feet, as cries of protest rang around the room. Emmett frowned and looked at Ryker, who seemed resigned almost.

"What is it?" he said over the noise.

"Silence," Ryker demanded, and everyone immediately stopped talking.

"Have you lost your mind?" The Panthera nearly vibrated with fury as she stood, but Emmett stood in shock as he realized she wasn't talking to him but to Barry.

"What sort of retribution?" Emmett pushed.

Barry's satisfaction was almost palpable. "You are a panther, and because the Panthera has visited and therefore formally acknowledged you as clan, I have the right to retribution in a formal fight...to the death."

Ryker stepped in front of Emmett, putting himself between Emmett and all the panthers. "And as his alpha, I have the right to accept on his behalf."

"No." Barry paled. "You can't do that."

"Yes, he can," the Panthera said resignedly. "Which you would know if you cared anything about the history of our species, not just how much money you can make out of it."

Emmett shook his head and tugged frantically at Ryker's arm. "What does that mean? I don't want—" But Ryker rounded on Emmett and shook his head. Emmett shut up immediately, realizing that Ryker had tried to stop him before, and this was why. Ryker cupped Emmett's cheek.

"It will be fine."

"No, I recant," Barry started sputtering. "I have no argument with the alpha."

BABY AND THE WOLF

"I don't accept," Ryker said. "You have insulted my mate, and as such, I would demand retribution anyway." Then, to Emmett's horror, Ryker stalked to the door.

"Chrissy," Emmett said desperately. "You have to stop him."

Chrissy just shook her head. "I cannot stop the alpha from a righteous challenge. He defends his mate."

Red and Fox had already followed Ryker. Emmett looked at his grandmother. "You have to stop this, please."

"I cannot," she whispered and turned to go outside. "All I can do is witness."

Emmett ducked past everyone and ran after Ryker. "Ryker, no, please." Ryker rounded on him, and he came to a sudden stop. "I didn't mean for this to happen. I don't want you—" But Ryker pressed a finger over his lips to silence him, then kissed them.

"Don't worry." Then he turned and pulled his shirt off over his head.

"Ryker!"

Chrissy caught Emmett's hand and pulled him back. "Emmett, he needs to focus."

"But what's he doing? I don't want this. He might get hurt." Emmett tugged at his arm, but Chrissy was amazingly strong.

Chrissy turned into him. "Emmett. He's a strong wolf. You have to support him. Don't shame him by making it sound like you doubt he would win." Emmett stilled, protests battering his mind. "He needs to know you trust him. He's alpha," she said as if that explained everything. She waited until Emmett nodded, then let go. Ryker had already toed off his boots and was unbuttoning his pants.

Looking like he was going to pee himself, Barry reluctantly did the same.

Taking a deep breath, Emmett walked to where Ryker stood, picked up his shirt, and held his hand out for his pants. It was the closest thing he could think of to demonstrate his loyalty...*and his love*, because he did love Ryker with everything in him. Why had he never said it?

Ryker grinned and pulled him in for a kiss. Emmett went willingly and

143

VICTORIA SUE

let the big wolf maul his mouth, prepared—even with an audience—to get lost in his touch.

"Alpha," Chrissy screamed, and something slammed into Emmett so hard he was sprawled on the ground before he knew what had happened.

Shouts, growls, snarls, and a blur of claws and teeth as a massive black panther leaped onto Ryker's back before he was fully shifted. Emmett heard the answering snarl, but not before he saw the blood as Ryker's flesh ripped. Hands reached for Emmett and pulled him away just before the panther slammed the wolf down hard, his jaws going for Ryker's throat.

Emmett stumbled again as Chrissy and Fox got him out of the way, and he looked back in terror as the wolf just managed to avoid the panther's jaws a second time.

"Fuck, he's big," Red muttered unnecessarily.

Emmett clasped Chrissy's hand—terrified to watch but unable to look away. Another snarl and more blood splattered the ground. Emmett thought his heart was going to stop. They were moving so fast he couldn't even see which animal the blood was coming from. Then he heard the pained cry from Ryker as Barry fastened his jaws onto his shoulder blade, but he somehow managed to twist at the last second to stop Barry from getting his teeth on his neck and jump away. Emmett could barely breathe. Both animals were covered in blood. Barry had a gash on his side, and the fur on Ryker's back glistened. They both looked exhausted, and they each prowled, never taking their eyes off each other.

Then the panther leaped, and for an interminable second, Emmett thought Ryker wasn't going to move. He heard the sharp inhale from Chrissy, and just as it looked like Barry would barrel right into Ryker, Ryker dived, rolled, and clawed Barry's belly. Blood and guts gushed everywhere, and Emmett turned his head before he threw up. As long as he lived, Emmett never wanted to hear such a cry of agony ever again. Then, because he couldn't bear not to look, he saw Ryker stagger to his feet as a human and bend to Barry. "Shift," he yelled and glanced up at the Panthera. She nodded to one of her claw, and he strode purposefully to Barry. Emmett thought he was going to make him shift somehow, but the man bent, took ahold of the panther's head, and twisted it sharply.

144

BABY AND THE WOLF

The resounding crack seemed almost deafening. Barry immediately shifted into a human, but he lay still, his head at an awkward angle. The other panther had just finished him off on the order of the Panthera. Killed him, when Ryker wouldn't have, even though Barry would have killed Ryker.

Ryker. Emmett's feet got themselves unglued, and he ran at Ryker, getting there a moment before the other wolves. Ryker opened his arms before Emmett slammed into him, and finally Emmett was crying. "Don't you ever scare the shit out of me like that again," he mumbled, but quietly so he wouldn't embarrass him.

Ryker just nodded, and for a moment, it was just them. "Are you okay? He slammed into me so fast I knocked you over. We'll get Marco to check you out."

Emmett clung onto Ryker. "You saved my life. If you hadn't gotten me out of the way, he'd have had me." Emmett clung to Ryker, but he knew he had to face the panthers eventually, so he turned. Two men were covering Barry's body with a sheet, and the third opened the trunk.

Emmett swallowed, nausea trying to overwhelm him.

"Emmett?"

He turned to look at his grandmother, completely unsure of how he felt.

"He shamed himself and us all by attacking when the omega was present," she offered as an explanation, and Emmett was stunned. She doubted she ever explained herself. "I am still investigating how he squandered his money and then tried to spend your mother's in return for his so-called care. I would never have hurt Josephine. It was why I stayed away. You have a fine alpha, and sometime—" She hesitated. "Sometime, I would like to get to know you and the pup."

He followed her gaze to his belly, remembered that the Panthera could tell if someone was pregnant, even though it was getting a little obvious now, and looked into her eyes. He didn't know what had gone wrong between his mom and her mother, but maybe it was time to put a lot of things to rest. "I'm not interested in the clan, but I think I'd like to get to know my mom's family."

She smiled, her eyes glittering with unshed moisture, then looked at Ryker. "The Blue Ridge pack has my clan's gratitude and support." Emmett gazed at Ryker, then moved slightly to block him because Ryker was very naked, and this woman was his grandmother. Then she walked to her car as if nothing had happened.

Emmett watched as they drove away. He turned and handed Ryker his pants, which somehow he had managed to keep ahold of.

Ryker put them on but didn't take his eyes off Emmett. "I need a shower."

"You two go to the cabin," Chrissy said. "I'll make sure all the pups are okay and keep Calvin here until you come for him."

Emmett nodded and turned to Ryker. "Are you okay?"

"I'm fine. Shifted." He waved a hand at himself.

"I have two things I want to say," Emmett said seriously, and Ryker stilled. He stayed silent, but Emmett knew somehow he expected bad news. "First, I'm sorry. Me and my big mouth nearly got you killed." His lip wobbled a little on the last word, and Ryker pulled him into the comfort of his arms.

"Don't go, *please*," Ryker mumbled into his hair.

Emmett pushed away so he could look at Ryker. "Go? Where am I going?"

Ryker searched Emmett's face, and Emmett met his eyes. "You're rich if you want to be. You have a whole new family. I don't know what I'm doing most of the time and *umpff*."

Emmett launched himself at Ryker. "I love you, and I'm going nowhere."

Ryker tightened his hold, and Emmett sighed in delight. "I love you more," Ryker said throatily. "You're my life."

Emmett kissed him thoroughly for that admission and he could feel Ryker's approval poking his belly. "Let's get a shower while Calvin is otherwise occupied." He waggled his eyebrows suggestively.

Ryker didn't need to be asked twice.

CHAPTER FIFTEEN

SHOWER SEX WAS his favorite thing, Emmett decided when Ryker eventually tucked him into bed for another nap. Calvin was fine and Ryker had gammas patrolling. He didn't doze for long, though, because he had promised to see Kai. So, when he woke up, he got dressed and opened the cabin door to see a medium-sized tan wolf gazing at him. He thought he was one of Nema's sons, but he didn't know which. "Aldred?"

The wolf blinked up at him, panting.

"No? Rhys?" He thought Rhys was the eldest. The wolf whined and sat, so Emmett took that as a yes. "Are you my escort?" The wolf whined again, and Emmett wondered if they could get some sort of growl language going. One yip for yes, maybe. He set off to the pack house and walked right into the kitchen, only to nearly be mowed down by a whirlwind called Calvin.

"Are you all right? Chrissy said you were, but you were tired. Is the baby okay? Is it hungry? I drew a picture."

Emmett chuckled and returned the hug, then watched Calvin go back to happily playing with Joshua. He had lost a lot of his wariness in the last few weeks, didn't automatically assume if Emmett was out of sight he should worry.

"Brownies?" Emmett whispered, sidling up to Dinah.

She rolled her eyes. "There's plenty." She handed him a plastic tub.

Emmett grinned and squeezed her shoulders. "Thanks, Nana."

Dinah flushed but looked pleased and shooed him away. He walked up to Kai's door and put up his hand to knock, hearing someone say loudly, "This is completely irresponsible." Without thinking, he pushed the door open to see Kai glaring at Marco, Kai's half-packed suitcase on the bed.

Marco looked up, scowling. "Maybe you can talk some sense into him." Then he pushed past Emmett, slamming the door shut on his way out.

Emmett turned to Kai. "What are you doing?"

"What does it look like?" Kai retorted and blinked furiously. Emmett steered him gently to a seat.

"Talk to me."

"I'm leaving for Meridian, Mississippi, in the morning." Kai chewed his lip. "I have no choice." He glanced at the closed door. "At least there I have someone who *wants* to mate with me," he said bitterly.

Emmett's ears pricked up at Kai's tone. Someone? Kai pressed both his lips together. "I don't trust myself to know it's real, and I can't wait around to find out. I don't know what those panthers did to him, but it messed with his head. He says he'd be no good as anyone's mate."

Marco. It was Marco. "It didn't sound as if he wanted you to leave though," Emmett said encouragingly.

Kai shrugged. "I can't wait until the pup's born. Since the cave rescue, some of the other omegas have told me they've gotten similar requests for introductions. If the shifter world knows where we are, I don't trust my former alpha not to come for the pup. He might not have wanted me, but he'd definitely want him."

"I'm sorry, Kai."

He sniffed. "There's nothing you can do. I need to mate to protect him, and once that's done, we're both safe." He smiled, but Emmett could see it was forced. "My alpha is sending a car for me in the morning." Kai stood and came over. "But I want to say goodbye now. Please don't be there to see me off."

"Kai," Emmett whispered. "But—"

Kai laid a gentle finger over Emmett's lips and kissed his cheek.

"Please, for me. And we will be able to call each other." He nodded to his phone on the dresser.

"Promise me you'll let me know how you're doing?"

Kai nodded, then stepped back and made a shooing motion with his hand. "You have to go. I can't cry again."

Emmett swallowed down the lump in his throat and simply left. He rounded the corner and nearly ran into Marco.

"He's leaving in the morning. Can't you—"

"No," Marco whispered and turned and headed for the main door.

"What's wrong, love?" Emmett turned around to see Ryker.

He blew out a breath. "Kai's leaving in the morning, and he wants Marco to ask him to stay. And not because of his health," Emmett added.

"Damn," Ryker said. "I didn't see that coming." He put an arm around Emmett's shoulders. "I'm sorry." Emmett leaned into Ryker. "I spoke to Kai."

"You did?" Emmett asked hopefully.

"I can't stop him, and he's made up his mind. I tried."

Emmett nodded. Kai had said he was worried about his baby, but he thought it was that he simply didn't trust himself or his own feelings. If he really wanted to, he could stay.

"Do you want to come and tell me what you think of our latest round of pack applications?"

Emmett nodded disconsolately and let Ryker steer him into the office. Chrissy and Red were already there. They were discussing plans for a school—well, a schoolroom—but he thought it was important to have a separate space. Emmett had just decided he was hungry and ought to check on Calvin when Fox strode into the room. The look he shot Emmett made the breath catch in his throat.

"I just took a call from the Mills River pack alpha. They have a wolf omega down there who belongs to a pack over in Tennessee. Apparently he escaped from Mills River four years ago after being beaten and left for dead." He glanced at Emmett, eyes full of apology, and Emmett knew before the wolf had even opened his mouth what he was going to say. "He claims Calvin is his son, and he wants him back."

Emmett felt like the words were buzzing like insects in his head. Buzzing but not landing, so he couldn't take them in. He put a hand to his chest as if he could stop the sudden pain. Blindly, he took a step toward the door. He could have carried on to the forest, but Ryker would have just come after him.

"Where is he?" Ryker ground out.

"On his way. About another hour."

"But how will we know?" Emmett suddenly thought. "You said there were no records."

"Scent," Chrissy said quietly. "He and Calvin will share a scent. Is he on his own?"

"There's an enforcer with him, not a mate," Fox said. "The omega's name is Michael."

Emmett grasped the idea eagerly. "If he is on his own, he might want to join this pack." Then he wouldn't lose Calvin. He could still see him. He rubbed the mound on his belly absently and was immediately ashamed. How would he feel if Calvin had been his and he'd been missing for the last four years? Calvin's dad would be just as heartbroken. He headed to the kitchen. Calvin was playing with Joshua and Mira as usual. Damien, their omega, was sitting with a cup of coffee and watching over them. He looked up, smiling as Emmett came back in. It took everything in Emmett not to reach over and grab Calvin, but he sat down instead. The kids were laughing and snacking on cut-up fruit and sandwiches, vroom-vrooming their cars and trucks around the floor. He was confident they were making enough noise that they wouldn't take any notice of what he said if he spoke softly.

"Damien, do you know an omega called Michael?"

Damien shook his head and lowered his voice to match Emmett's. "Do you mean from the Mills River pack?" Emmett had gotten quite friendly with Damien, and he doubted he would lie. Damien wanted to stay here with his kids.

"He left there four years ago. He belongs to a pack in Tennessee now."

BABY AND THE WOLF

Damien shook his head. "No, sorry. Unless we were in the same omega house, we wouldn't have met. There's a chance I might have seen him, but I'm not an alpha, obviously."

Emmett wrinkled his brow. "What's that got to do with it?"

"Alpha wolves can recognize the scent of all their pack. They'd only have to meet them once." He shrugged. "It's an alpha thing. Good when the alpha is protective, awkward if that isn't the case."

Emmett nodded. He was doing his best to get the omegas together and get to know them, but they were all still nervous. Louis just looked terrified every time Emmett tried to talk to him.

"Is he wanting to join this pack?"

"I don't know. He wants something else at the moment." Emmett tipped his head at Calvin, and Damien's eyes widened.

"Ask Darriel."

Emmett nodded and stood just as Chrissy came back into the kitchen. Emmett squeezed Damien's hand and went to meet her.

"Are you okay, Emmett?" She looked as sickened as he felt.

"I'm going to speak to Darriel. See if he has heard of him. Damien hasn't. Can you ask the others?"

"Good idea." Chrissy walked away to where the other omegas' rooms were. He headed over to Darriel's room and knocked.

Marco opened the door and smiled stiffly.

"Everything looks okay," Darriel said, nodding to the ultrasound Marco was just packing away. He winced. "I'm not out of the woods, obviously, but they both seem fine for the moment."

Emmett breathed a happy sigh for Darriel and sat in the chair by the bed. Marco left them to it.

"What's the matter?" Darriel asked. "You look worried."

Emmett opened his mouth to say but had to close it quickly when his throat ached. He put a hand to his mouth. Darriel silently took the other one and waited until Emmett got himself together. "Calvin's omega is on his way here."

Darriel's eyebrows shot up. "Who?"

"Michael? I don't know his last name."

"He might not have one. If he's from my old pack, we never needed one. Sometimes we had to use the pack name. Tell me."

"I'm trying to find out if anyone knows him. I—" His throat closed again.

"You don't want to let Calvin go, but at the same time, you understand how an omega would feel," Darriel said gently.

Emmett nodded and blinked rapidly. "Is that really bad?"

"Of course not. What sort of omega is he?"

"Wolf."

Darriel nodded. "So, they'll know, then. Is there any chance he might stay here?"

Emmett shot him a watery smile. "I hope so." But if he didn't, there would be nothing Emmett could do. He glanced at Darriel. "You look better."

"Marco says if I'm okay tomorrow, I can get up." He squeezed Emmett's hand. "I'm sure it will be okay."

Emmett took a deep breath and stood. He nodded. "I'll come back later."

Ryker met him as soon as he left Darriel's, and Emmett stepped right into his outstretched arms. "None of the omegas Chrissy has spoken to remember a Michael, but that's not unusual, unfortunately. And the pack is closed. The alpha from Mills River hasn't had any contact with them."

"What does closed mean?" Emmett mumbled against Ryker's shirt.

"No communication with the outside world. No telephones. Definitely no Wi-Fi. Fox is trying to make a few calls, but the scouts told me their car passed them fifteen minutes ago. They'll be here any moment."

"If it's true, what will happen?"

Ryker swallowed audibly. "If it's true, I am going to do my best to get him to stay, but I cannot force him."

Emmett gazed up at Ryker. "Are you saying he can just take Calvin and there's nothing we can do?"

Ryker didn't answer for a moment. "Packs are autonomous. There's no such thing as family services for shifters, and it's only because Mills River has changed their alpha that Michael could ask this. He would have known

BABY AND THE WOLF

he couldn't have gotten Calvin before now. I could challenge the enforcer if he tries anything, but I can't physically detain an omega. Well, I could, but—"

"I wouldn't ask you to," Emmett acknowledged. He couldn't make Ryker into the same sort of monster the old alpha from Mills River was. Calvin deserved his family. What his omega had gone through must be unimaginable.

"How about you go get the meeting room ready? I'm going to try and part Calvin from his friends. Make sure his shirt is clean. See if he needs the bathroom." Except Emmett's voice cracked on the last word, and Ryker growled, pulling him close.

"We will talk to them first. If we establish they are who they say they are, I'll come and find you both."

Emmett nodded. "What do I say to Calvin?"

"If he's his omega, Calvin will recognize his scent. You won't need to say anything." Ryker winced. "Maybe just say we have a friend from his old pack who wants to meet him?"

Emmett stepped back and headed to the kitchen. Calvin was putting the cars away with the other two, and all three kids were yawning. Emmett opened his arms, and Calvin rushed into them. Emmett closed his eyes and for a moment hugged him tight. Then Calvin wriggled. "There's someone who wants to meet you. We think he might be a friend of your omega." He just couldn't take Calvin into the room without saying something.

"A friend?" Calvin asked curiously.

"Mm-hmm," Emmett agreed and let Calvin down and held out his hand. "Let's go home—" He swallowed and amended. "Let's go back to our room and change your T-shirt and make sure your hands are clean, huh?"

"'Kay," Calvin agreed happily, and all the way back, he chatted excitedly about the gamma cadet board and how he was doing, and did Emmett think Ryker would let Joshua and Mira be gamma cadets. Emmett ignored the tightness in his throat and assured Calvin he would. It didn't seem to take any time at all. At the last moment before they went back, Emmett picked up the rabbit from Calvin's little bed. "Maybe your friend would like to meet him?"

Calvin nodded and held him tight. Emmett took his other hand, and they walked back. Chrissy looked up from where she was standing outside the room waiting for them. He'd seen the truck at the entrance, so he knew they were here, and one look at her face sent his heart into his boots. He wasn't going to get Calvin upset though, and they followed Chrissy into the small meeting room.

Emmett noticed the two men right away, despite Ryker drawing both he and Calvin close. The bigger of the two—obviously the enforcer—looked like a poster boy for the mafia. He had thought Ryker was big, but this guy was massive. He also didn't look especially happy to be here. Emmett forced himself to look at the omega and was surprised to see quite a tall man. All the omegas he had seen were a lot smaller, but he guessed that was on him for stereotyping. The omega glanced at Calvin, then over at the bigger man.

The enforcer stood. "We request formal identification."

Calvin shrank into Emmett's side when the enforcer spoke, and Emmett didn't blame him. If he was trying to be intimidating, it was working. Emmett sat down next to Ryker and pulled Calvin onto his knee. He looked at the omega. "Hi, I'm Emmett, and this is Calvin. You're Michael?"

Michael nodded, and the enforcer—reluctantly—sat down. He nodded to the omega. "You need to be sure."

Michael stood, his face expressionless, and walked around to Calvin. He bent down, and Emmett could see his nostrils flaring as he inhaled. Michael cocked his head and regarded Calvin steadily. "Do you recognize me?"

Calvin inhaled, and Emmett could have cried. It was such an automatic reaction. He doubted if Calvin even knew he was doing it. Calvin wrinkled his nose a little, but he nodded cautiously, and Emmett's heart thudded.

Michael turned to Ryker. "He's mine, and I petition for his return."

Ryker hesitated. "We insist on three confirmations."

Emmett watched, no idea what Ryker meant, but he saw Ryker inhale slowly, then back off. Fox went next, then Chrissy. Emmett tightened his arms around Calvin. He dare not look at Ryker.

"Emmett?" Ryker said gently.

Emmett closed his eyes against the horror. He knew what that apologetic tone meant. He swallowed and opened his eyes, brushed a kiss on the top of Calvin's head, and smiled brightly at Michael.

"Maybe we could all get some supper? I'm sure—"

"No," the enforcer cut him off. "We have a long drive, and our alpha expects us back tonight."

Emmett gaped.

Michael bent down and lifted Calvin off Emmett's lap, and for a second he was too shocked to protest. Standing, Calvin took a step back to Emmett automatically, but Michael firmed his grip, stopping him. "We should go. I don't think it's fair on the pup to linger."

"But surely—"

"It's a long drive," Ryker cut in. "We'd be happy to offer you somewhere to stay tonight."

"And upset the pup further?" Michael asked, a challenge in his tone. Calvin tried to wriggle out of his grasp.

"Emmett." His voice wobbled, and he looked at Ryker. "Alpha?"

"He's not your alpha, pup," the enforcer said bluntly, and Calvin started struggling.

"No." He tried to get free. "I want Emmett." And he burst into tears.

Michael simply scooped him up. "We need to go. This isn't fair."

Emmett shook, tears rolling down his own face. He couldn't do this. Pain like nothing he'd ever felt before clasped his chest in tight fingers. Calvin was full-on screaming and struggling. Emmett stood, not knowing what to do, and reached out to pass him the rabbit.

Michael shook his head. "It has your scent. I would prefer him not to have that."

Emmett choked out another sob as they walked from the room, Calvin's wails were so loud the whole pack could hear. Emmett took a step, but Ryker stood and blocked him. He wrapped Emmett up tightly in his arms while Emmett struggled, but when he heard the car engine start, he turned his head into Ryker's chest and sobbed, crying as he felt his heart shatter into a million different pieces.

CHAPTER SIXTEEN

FORTY-EIGHT HOURS LATER, Ryker worried Emmett was going to make himself sick. He wasn't eating nearly enough, and all he seemed to want to do was sleep. He'd also headed to their old cabin and refused to sleep in the pack house. Marco didn't seem to be able to help. He'd offered him a scan, but that had just set him off again. Kai had gone as planned but had made sure Ryker had his phone number and email. They'd tried to contact the pack in Tennessee to find out how Calvin was, but there was no way to make contact other than through the shifter council, and they just said no laws had been broken, so they couldn't interfere. Ryker knew Emmett wouldn't even start to settle until he knew Calvin was adjusting. He didn't want his last memory of him to be a screaming child practically ripped from his arms.

Ryker was at least happy with his new pack members, including the teacher, whose wife immediately pitched in to help Dinah, and his three sons, one of whom—Nema admitted—was an omega and the reason he had been wanting to leave his old pack. Neither Nema nor his wife trusted their old alpha around their youngest, Teo. He had kept his hands off the male omegas born to mated couples, but Nema hadn't trusted the alpha, and

VICTORIA SUE

Isabelle, his wife, had been frantic. The new alpha might be better but they wanted a change.

Their new cabin was ready, but when he'd mentioned it to Emmett, Emmett had burst into tears, and he knew why. The cabin had three bedrooms with room for more to be added if he needed, but the fact there was just the two of them at the moment weighed heavily on them both. It was just to the side of the pack house. They were there in case they were needed, but it gave them the small amount of privacy he'd originally wanted.

It wouldn't have been as bad if they could have at least gotten ahold of someone at Michael's pack, and after another day with a tearful Emmett, Ryker grabbed Red, and they got in the truck. It would take them nearly two hours to get to Mills River. The alpha might not know anything about the Catoosa pack in Tennessee, but he was desperate. Marco was going to keep an eye on Emmett, and Darriel was planning on keeping him company. He hoped talking about their pregnancies might cheer Emmett up even a little bit. He wasn't eating properly, and while he spent every night in Ryker's arms, it seemed like he wasn't really there. Marco said it was grief. For all intents and purposes, they'd lost a child. He'd even asked Ryker how *he* was, but he couldn't think about himself when he was too worried about Emmett.

And he couldn't let it go any longer.

Gammas met them at the boundary, and after saying who they were and requesting to see the alpha, they were waved through. Two enforcers met them at the pack house, and they were escorted inside. Ryker shot a look at Red. This pack clearly had money. The pack house itself was like a five-star hotel.

They were shown into an office, and Ryker was surprised to see the young man that greeted them. "Alpha?"

"Jered," he confirmed.

"Ryker, and this is my beta, Red."

"What can I do for you? How's Darriel?"

"Much better. Thanks for letting him stay until we could move him."

Jered nodded. "It's fine. Makes me feel like less of a shit for them having to leave."

Ryker eyed him carefully. "I get the impression you're between a rock and a hard place."

"Like you wouldn't believe," Jered said with feeling. "Can I offer you coffee?"

Ryker shook his head. "We're hoping you might be able to help us with the omega Michael that came to us from the pack in Tennessee."

Jered crossed his arms and leaned against the desk. "In what way?"

Ryker told him about Emmett, Calvin, and the cave rescue.

Jered paled. "Shit. I wish I had been able to get my hands on that bastard Riggs, but one fight was enough."

"Fight?"

"I challenged my father."

Shit. Ryker hadn't known that and couldn't imagine what he was going through. He knew the challenge would have been bloody. To fight his father to the death was unimaginable. At least he hadn't had to do that. Jered seemed matter of fact, but Ryker knew he would be anything but. "I'm desperate, quite frankly. Three of us confirmed the scent."

"You do know that can also be an indication of close family?"

Ryker turned at the voice and looked at the man who was standing at the door.

The wolf put out his hand. "Morgan. I'm the alpha's beta commander."

"It's unlikely though," Red pointed out after shaking hands. "I mean, what are the chances they even found out about Calvin after seven years? Surely with the omega houses being the mess they were, only Calvin's omega would know who he was."

"Very slim."

Jered turned to Morgan. "Do we have any records on this Michael?"

"I looked earlier when they arrived here asking about the pup." He walked to the new-looking computer on the desk. "You know I've been wading through what records we have, which isn't many, but a Michael and Steven Brand were born—twins—nineteen years ago. They were both omegas according to the records. Very unusual."

A cold chill ran up and down Ryker's spine. "And Steven isn't here now?"

Morgan shook his head. "No, I don't think so. Neive might know though?" He glanced at Jered.

"Possibly. I don't remember twins, but if they were omegas, even my uncle tended to keep those families separate, and he had over two thousand wolves."

"Neive?" Ryker prodded.

"One of the older pack mothers back when I was a pup," Jered explained. He nodded to Morgan, and Morgan left the room. He rubbed his face. "The whole thing's a mess. My uncle was very traditional, but he wasn't the monster my father was."

Ryker didn't respond. There was a world of pain in that one word "monster."

"He wouldn't have treated the male omegas like my father did, but he also wouldn't have allowed someone like your human partner to land a helicopter on his land." Jered smiled, and for the first time, Ryker grinned ruefully.

"Zeke is a force of nature. He's also my mate's father."

Jered's eyebrows rose. "I don't have to worry about security, then."

Ryker shook his head. "He's kept our secrets for a long time."

The door opened, and Morgan came back in with an older female. She looked about seventy in human years, but that could mean she was easily thirty years older or more.

"Pack mother," Jered greeted her respectfully.

"Alpha," she returned, smiling, and allowed Morgan to help her to the seat by the desk. She inhaled and fixed a stare on Ryker, then turned to Jered. "What is it you need of me?"

Jared spoke. "We're trying to find out about twins. One called Michael. According to the records, he was born—"

"On the eve of the pink supermoon eighteen, no, nineteen years ago," Neive interrupted. "His brother, Steven, was born seven minutes later. They were a new family just arrived, so I never got the chance to examine the mother before she labored."

Ryker knew that some pack mothers were said to be able to recall the details of every pup they had helped to birth, but it was more a legend. He'd never actually met one that could. "Do you know if they are still here?"

Morgan glanced at Ryker. "We have at least two hundred undocumented wolves, and the records we have are hopelessly out of date."

"No," Neive said. "There was a fight. Michael killed Steven when they were fifteen."

Red shot a stunned look at Ryker. "An omega killed another wolf?"

"I've never heard of an omega involved in a fight to the death," Jered agreed.

"No, he was the one killed. Steven," Neive confirmed.

Morgan frowned. "But Michael was an omega—"

Neive scoffed. "No, he wasn't, or not technically. He exhibited all the omega tendencies exactly like his brother except maybe a few inches of extra height, but he didn't have the necessary biology to get pregnant and carry a pup even though he never shifted. He was what in the olden days would be termed a mar-wolf—those wolves that through mixed breeding can never shift and aren't omegas either. Of course, we didn't have anything like the modern equipment the humans have, but every pack mother can recognize an omega shortly after birth. Steven was an omega, and he'd already caught the attention of one of the gammas. He'd even had a few pre-heats by the time he was in his teens. Michael was jealous. His father was disappointed because once he didn't have the excuse of being an omega, he was expected to toughen up, especially as his father was one of the alpha's enforcers, but when he reached fifteen and never shifted..." She shrugged. "In a traditional pack, it is considered a sign of weakness, as you know. That, plus his mother fussed over Steven because after the birth, she was damaged and could have no more pups. Steven was her one chance of getting grandbabies, which led to resentment."

"And they fought?" Ryker prodded.

Neive nodded. "Like I said, Steven drew the attention of one of the gammas. Michael was jealous, and they got into an argument. I don't think Michael was trying to kill his brother. They were tussling and fell off the ledge that ran around the woods. Steven hit his head on a rock and died instantly. As an omega, he was unable to shift, of course."

"And what happened?" Ryker asked.

"The alpha banished Michael after two of his gammas meted out punishment. His mother—Chevanne—was heartbroken. She killed herself a month later. His father became a gamma and then a beta. I understand he's not a pack member now."

"It still makes no sense though," Ryker said in frustration. "Why would Michael claim Calvin? He passed three scent tests."

Neive shook her head. "If he did, then he has to have very close familial ties. Where did he say he was from?"

"Catoosa pack, Tennessee."

"Catoosa pack have had their own problems recently," Morgan said. "In danger of losing some of their land."

"You know them? We can't get in touch at all," Red commented.

"None of which explains why Michael would claim a pup when he isn't even his omega," Ryker said in frustration. "You said his father isn't here any longer?"

"And good riddance," Neive said dryly. "Disgusting how he treated Chevanne, but what he did with those omegas was revolting. I felt sorry for him when he lost his mate, but I soon changed my opinion."

Ryker froze, his pulse beating loudly in his ears. "What was his father's name? The beta?"

"Riggs," Neive said.

"Fuck," Ryker spat out.

"My father let some of his enforcers have the omegas as a reward," Jered said. "He used to insist on it only after he had already gotten them pregnant, but it's not impossible to think he made a mistake and Riggs got one of them pregnant."

Pregnant.

"I wouldn't be surprised if Riggs was the father half the time," Jered added.

That was the connection. Everything in Ryker screamed it was. "No wonder Calvin and Michael share a scent. He's Calvin's half-brother." *And he's fuck knows where with Calvin.* Ryker's heart was pounding so loudly he missed the next thing Jered said.

"And the omegas were drugged. It was likely they didn't know," Morgan agreed.

They all thanked Neive when the old pack mother got up to leave.

Ryker was still reeling from finding out Riggs was Calvin's father.

"There's something else," Jered said quietly after Neive had gone, and he shared a look with Morgan.

Ryker raised his eyebrows. "Something else?"

"There are a lot of omegas missing, and we were approached yesterday by an alpha in Kentucky to ask if we had any omegas for sale. He was surprised to discover we don't do that anymore."

Ryker closed his eyes as nausea threatened him.

"And I know for a fact that my father would never get rid of an omega," Jered said.

"You think Riggs is behind this?" But he knew. Riggs had been doing this for a long time. Maybe this was even the scheme Riggs and his father were involved with. As a pack alpha, his father would want to keep the omegas, but once it was no longer his pack, it would have been all about the money. He'd thought it was guns or drugs, but the more he learned, he realized he'd been wrong.

"It sounds like it," Jered admitted. "And my father definitely wouldn't sell an omega, he would consider them too valuable, as I said. I could see Riggs doing it though. He was a greedy bastard."

Ryker's knees nearly gave way. He'd thought this was about revenge, but it wasn't. Riggs didn't give a shit about Ryker. This was about money, pure and simple. They were going to *sell* omegas. They'd been selling omegas for years. "We need to get back," Ryker croaked out.

"But how would Riggs even know you had Calvin?" Morgan asked. "He could be anywhere."

Not if he had been responsible for putting them in the cave in the first place. Riggs knew exactly where they were.

"If Riggs is behind this, I am more than happy to provide you all the enforcers you need to get the pup back." Jered shrugged. "I'm happy to

VICTORIA SUE

help either way. I'm sick of packs being in competition, and I hear you do good work."

Ryker nodded. He wanted to set off to Tennessee now, but they needed a team, and they needed the pack to be protected while they were away. "I'm going back to arrange my team. I'll call you, but I intend to leave tonight."

Jered nodded.

"Good luck," Morgan and Jered said almost simultaneously.

He was definitely going to need it.

* * *

EMMETT OPENED his eyes and nearly closed them again as hurt tore through him at the silence. There was no puff of warm air at his neck, no heavy arm slung so protectively over him. No sound of little snores or even childish giggles as Ryker put his cadet through his paces outside. How a seven-year-old was supposed to stalk a rabbit in human form was beyond him, but that was the sight that had greeted him one day last week when he'd taken his tea outside. Ryker was born to be a dad. The huge grumpy alpha turned into a marshmallow around Calvin, and as Emmett had rested his hand on his growing bump, he knew Ryker would have lots of love and care to give their baby. He'd wanted a family for so long, and for a moment, life had been perfect.

He didn't begrudge Michael. He'd just seemed so stiff and cold, and Calvin had been terrified. Had a quick, ripping-the-Band-Aid-off approach been the right thing to do? Calvin was young, and as much as Emmett hated to admit it, he would forget Emmett when he got settled with his new family. Emmett pulled a pillow over his head to muffle a sob in case Ryker was nearby. He didn't know how he would bear it, but then he put his hand protectively over his belly and stilled at the fluttering inside him. More tears leaked, but it was the nudge he needed.

He threw back the covers. He'd neglected everyone, especially Darriel. He'd seen Darriel twice, but his dad seemed to be spending a lot of time with him, so that was good. He guessed anyway, although it made things

BABY AND THE WOLF

awkward, and he hoped when Darriel had recovered, he wasn't going to break his dad's heart.

He knew Ryker had to leave to go somewhere with Red. He couldn't even remember where he said he was going, and that was awful. He was supposed to be the alpha-mate and have responsibilities, but he'd just left getting the new omegas settled to Chrissy and Dinah. He was due to have a baby in seven weeks, and he'd given it hardly any thought. He knew Ryker wanted them to move to the new cabin, but he'd taken one look and dissolved into tears.

Calvin was where he should be, and Emmett needed to get his act together. He was going to get showered, force himself to eat something because he didn't want to go back to passing out, and then he was going to take a walk around the front of the pack house and go see his new cabin.

A half hour later, after managing half a bagel, some cheese, and ham, Emmett opened the cabin door to see a different wolf on guard. He smiled. "I'm going to the pack house." He walked there, entering the kitchen and seeing it was empty. Then suddenly he was angry. Angry with himself and angry with the whole world almost. He yanked the door back open, glad that the wolf had gone, and ran almost breathless to the trees, tears streaming down his face. Damien and he had been thinking of taking the kids to the creek at the bottom of the hill. He was determined Calvin would learn to swim. Emmett covered his face with his hands. It was over. He had to stop thinking of Calvin. He just didn't know how.

With zero warning, he was nearly yanked off his feet. A hand clamped over his mouth to stop any cry, and he was dragged into the trees. He felt something sharp press into his belly, and his heart just about stopped.

"You move or make one noise and I will push this knife in. I don't think I'll miss what you've got in there, huh?" He pressed the knife into his skin harder, and Emmett shook his head frantically. Who was it? The man kept the bruising grip on his arm and turned Emmett around.

"Who are you?" Emmett took in the barely dressed man.

The laugh was unexpected. "An old pal of Ryker's. I know your alpha's not here. Think I would have got within twenty feet of you if he had been?"

Emmett swallowed. The man was huge. He'd guess he was a shifter,

165

but either way, personal hygiene wasn't high on his list of priorities. "The enforcers will miss me when I don't get to the pack house."

The man grinned a mouthful of sharp teeth. "I think they'll be a while yet. Human hunters were spotted trying to get onto your land. It'll keep them busy for a while."

Emmett was sick of being played. "What do you want?" Maybe if he could keep him talking, Chrissy would come looking for him.

"I think it might be more a case of what you want."

Emmett's pulse picked up. "What do you mean?"

"I mean, I might have taken something about so high"—he raised his hand until it was just over three feet off the ground—"whines like a bitch. Doesn't seem to be happy with dear old dad."

By force of will, Emmett remained on his feet. "Who are you?"

"Call me Riggs."

Emmett really wished he hadn't eaten that bagel. He so didn't want it to make a reappearance. "But Michael..."

Riggs snorted his derision. "It's about time that useless pup of mine did something useful. He's been a waste of space for nearly twenty years."

Emmett couldn't process what was happening. Somehow this monster had his boy, and Ryker wasn't anywhere near to help.

"You come quietly now or the kid dies. You make any fuss, and the next time you see him, he won't be whining at anything because he won't have a throat to whine with."

CHAPTER SEVENTEEN

"WHAT DO YOU WANT TO DO?" Red asked as soon as they got back into the truck. "I mean, apart from going to get him, obviously."

Ryker huffed, not surprised that Red knew exactly what was going through his head. "What distance are we talking about?" He knew roughly.

"In the truck, three hours, but I'm not convinced he's there."

Ryker glanced over at him before Red drove through the pack entrance and headed home. "What do you mean?"

"I mean, how do we know Michael took him back to the pack? How do we even know they weren't making that up?"

A chill ran through Ryker. "We don't, I guess, although where else would they take him?" And the thought he might already be sold was too sickening to contemplate.

"Tell me about Riggs," Red said instead of answering his question.

"He was a gamma, eventually a beta until my father lost the pack. Zeke stopped him from killing me."

"Emmett's dad?" Red said in amazement.

Ryker nodded. "Riggs was corrupt even then, and he had his hand in a lot of illegal stuff. Main one being guns. I heard them arguing about the new alpha taking over, and they knew I'd heard. My father was drunk. He'd beaten my mom to death. Riggs had turned up after and he was furious. Not because he'd killed her, but because it might draw unwanted attention to them. My dad said Riggs owed him cash for covering for him, and I had to keep quiet. Dad shot me, but then Riggs finished him off. Head shot for my dad so he couldn't shift after fighting over the gun. He got me in the chest, and I shifted. Then he got me in the throat and the chest, and I was losing too much blood too quickly to do a double shift. He heard Zeke's truck and ran, assuming I was bleeding out. Zeke stopped the bleeding and waited with me until I could shift. He saved my life, then offered me a job."

"So, he's taken Calvin to punish you both?"

Ryker shook his head.

"I don't know how long he's been hanging around. It's been twenty years since I saw him, but the other day I caught a scent of something I recognized but couldn't remember where from. I'm guessing it was him." He hung his head, glad Red was driving.

"This isn't your fault," Red decreed.

But it was. For letting Riggs get the drop on him and for not recognizing Riggs's scent. What sort of alpha did that make him? "Where are we going to start if you think the pack's a load of bullshit?"

Red took a corner quickly and Ryker was glad he had his foot down. "I think he's close."

Ryker glanced over at him.

"I think he intended on coming back for the kids. I just think we got there before he got the chance."

"Another reason, we screwed his plans up."

"He's been watching the pack house since we took the kids back, right? We know he took them because they're omegas. He might have buyers for them, or maybe he wants his own pack. Male omegas are uncommon. Females are revered in pack circles, but it's like the older alphas don't know what to do with a male one, even though with the population problem, they need them. A lot of alphas see them as a means to an end, and I'm betting they're willing to pay a lot of cash for them."

"Fuck," Ryker groaned. "We might never get Calvin back." Emmett would be distraught.

Ryker's cell rang, and he answered it even though he didn't recognize the number.

"Well, well. You've been busy for a mixed bastard."

Ryker went cold all over. He recognized Riggs's voice right away. "What do you want?" Either he had called to gloat over having Calvin, or he wanted to negotiate. Zeke would put up any amount of money to make Emmett happy.

"Ryker?"

Ryker's heart slammed in his chest. "Emmett. Emmett, are you okay?" He heard the phone being taken away and a muffled cry.

"You hurt a single hair on his head—"

"Yeah, yeah," Riggs interrupted, sounding bored. "You know, originally I was just going to take the kid to fulfill my contract, but then I discovered who your mate was." He paused, obviously for theatrics.

Red glanced over and slowed the truck so they could listen.

"And dear old dad will pay a fortune to get him back. So, when I've decided how much I think he's worth, I'll be in touch. You'd just better hope I don't get bored with him first."

The line went dead, and every appalling scenario Ryker could think of looped around his brain on a never-ending circuit.

Red took the phone from him, but before he could make a call, the phone rang.

"This is Red."

"Red, Emmett's missing." Chrissy sounded frantic.

"We know," Red replied. "We'll be there in about forty minutes. Pull in every wolf we have." He hung up and looked at Ryker. "You need to call Zeke."

Ryker had the worst conversation of his life with Emmett's dad. Luckily, Zeke was already on his way to the pack house. When they pulled up, Fox, Red, and Chrissy were loading rescue equipment into their truck. Zeke arrived moments later. Marco came hurrying out with some equipment for the truck.

Zeke glanced over as Ryker got out. "I think you ought to call the Panthera."

Ryker came to an abrupt stop, and Zeke gazed at him. "Much as this kills me to say, if she's genuinely regretful about Josie and she wants to get to know Emmett, she'd be a good one to have in your corner. Shifted panthers are big bastards, as you know."

Ryker turned to Red. "Call Jered and ask if they will cover security for here. Ask if he's got anyone with caving experience."

He pulled his phone out to dial the number one of the Panthera's claw had left with Chrissy in case they could help.

"Why caving experience?" Red asked.

"Because he's been hiding around here. The kids were hidden in a cave. He can't risk them being scented by other wolves. It's a guess, but..."

Ryker pressed the number, not expecting the Panthera to answer, but he guessed she must have given them her private line. "Regina speaking."

Ryker's words nearly fell over themselves in his hurry to explain. Her harsh indrawn breath was the only sound she made until he was finished. "I have a team that will be perfect for this. They will be on their way within minutes. Where shall we meet?"

"The old escarpment. It used to be a picnic area. Outside hunting season, it's—"

"I know it," she interrupted. "And Ryker?"

"Yes," he whispered, waiting for condemnation.

"Thank you for calling me. We will do all we can to get your mate back safe and sound."

Wordlessly, Ryker got in the truck and half listened while Red brought everyone up to speed. He added what he knew of Riggs and then fell silent.

The escarpment, as the locals called it, was usually completely deserted out of hunting season. The main picnic area was now over sixty miles away, complete with a brand-new ranger station, an information center, and a gift shop. They all agreed that area was full of abandoned caves. If they had a chance to find them, it would be there. *If* they had a chance.

* * *

BABY AND THE WOLF

EMMETT DIDN'T KNOW where he was when he opened his eyes. Fear slammed into him as he automatically tried to reach to feel his baby bump, but found his hands were tied. He was freezing, and the air smelled damp. His head throbbed unmercifully since he'd come around a few minutes ago, and he shivered so much his teeth were chattering. He had no idea what Riggs had hit him with, but he remembered the brief flash of pain. Now, it just felt like someone was taking a hammer to his skull.

There was a little light from the cave entrance, but that still didn't tell him where they were, just that it was still daylight. He closed his eyes and breathed for a moment, trying to take stock of where he was. Then another memory slammed into him, and he opened them wide, ignoring the pain, and searched his prison. No Calvin. He didn't know whether to be relieved or worried that he wasn't here. Emmett pulled at his bound wrists in frustration. He couldn't move and... He held himself completely still. He'd been used to feeling little flutterings that had morphed into definite ripples and even tiny kicks, but he hadn't felt anything since he woke up. He stilled, his heart thumping loudly in his ears, but couldn't feel anything. Was the baby okay? He shivered. It was freezing in here.

He didn't have long to wonder, though, because he heard the telltale sound of scraping footsteps. He expected to see Riggs when he rounded the corner.

He didn't expect to see Calvin.

"Calvin? Sweetheart? Are you okay?" His questions came out in a rush, but Calvin cringed back toward Riggs as though...as though he was scared of Emmett. Emmett stopped, horrified, and for a moment didn't absorb what Riggs was saying.

"Poor kid, huh? Humans get this all the time. New pup and the others get shoved aside. I told him if your alpha had been at all bothered, he could have challenged Michael, but he didn't. He just let Michael walk out of there with Calvin because he knew you were going to present him with his own kid in a few weeks. I mean, there's no alpha I know that would want someone else's bastard when he's about to get his own."

"That's not true," Emmett said hotly. "Ryker couldn't fight an omega. It would be wrong."

"But Michael's not an omega. All alphas know that."

Emmett ignored Riggs. He knew what he was doing. "Calvin, sweetheart. Ryker is coming for us, you'll see." But Calvin wouldn't even look at him. He was even dressed in the same clothes as he had worn when Michael had taken him.

"Anyway, I expect Ryker to have called your dear old dad by now, so when he rounds up the cash, we can be on our way. We've got a pack to take us in, so no one can give either of us away."

Emmett dreaded the effect everything was having on the seven-year-old. Calvin didn't trust either Ryker or Emmett anymore. They had, in his mind, given him away, and the one constant—as evil a bastard as he was—was Riggs. Even though Emmett knew Riggs was lying, Calvin didn't.

Emmett kept his mouth closed with difficulty. When they got Calvin home was the time to start proving he was secure. He didn't know how he'd do it, but no one would take Calvin from him ever again. Shit, but tied to a wall wasn't the time to convince anyone.

Riggs's phone rang before he finished his next thought. Riggs frowned, then answered. He looked over at Emmett, complete shock morphing his features, and then he smiled. The self-satisfaction pouring off him would have made Emmett nauseous if he wasn't already.

"And just you, grandma," he snickered. "I smell so much as catnip and he dies." He nodded and clicked his phone off, then eyed Emmett with some amazement.

"Well, fuck me. Seems like you don't just have a dad with cash, your dear old mom had some too." He leaned forward. "And guess who's willing to pay for you to come home?"

The Panthera? Emmett was stunned and a little hopeful. "And Calvin. She'll pay for Calvin." Calvin had to know how much Emmett wanted him.

But Riggs shook his head and none too gently ruffled Calvin's hair. "Nah, I might keep the pup around. I mean, you're not gonna want him, and I'm building my own pack." But Riggs's voice was strained. There was something he wasn't saying.

"Of course I want him," Emmett said, wishing Calvin would look at him. He licked his dry lips. "Can I have some water, please?"

Riggs took a small water bottle off of his belt and handed it to Calvin. "Take it."

Calvin took the bottle with shaking hands and reluctantly carried it to Emmett. He still wouldn't look at him though. Emmett opened his mouth, and Calvin tipped a little too much in. Emmett tried to swallow but coughed sharply and gasped for breath. Calvin shot backward, dropping the bottle, and Riggs growled.

"Fucking idiot." He stepped forward, and Calvin ducked, obviously expecting a blow.

"It wasn't his fault," Emmett burst out as Riggs shoved Calvin and he staggered. "Leave him alone."

Riggs scoffed. "Pick it up."

Calvin seemed to curl into himself even more, but he did as he was asked and clutched at the bottle with trembling fingers.

Riggs gazed at Emmett, satisfaction obviously replacing irritation, and he smiled. He bent down, untied Emmett from the wall and hoisted him to his feet. His shoulders pulled unmercifully because his wrists were still tied. He was terrified Riggs would let him fall. If he did, he wouldn't be able to put his hands out to protect his belly.

He blinked against the sunlight as they got to the cave entrance and had no choice but to climb into the truck. Riggs pushed him onto his side on the floor in the back and told Calvin to get in the front. Emmett did his best to protect his bump, but it seemed that Riggs drove over every rut. His hands were still tied, so he tried with the little room he had to bring his knees up. After what seemed like an endless amount of time, he felt the truck slow and turn, then the engine die. He bit his lip hard, trying not to cry, but almost did from pain when Riggs pulled him from the truck.

"No tricks," Riggs spat out and pulled Emmett close to him so that Emmett was shielding Riggs's body. Riggs was also holding a gun.

Emmett gazed around a clearing, but his eyes widened when he saw the sleek black Lincoln and the woman who got out of it. Emmett stared in disbelief as he looked at his grandmother. She seemed to have aged forty years almost overnight. Gone was the makeup and the classic hairstyle, the three-inch heels and the Armani suit. She looked frail. In fact, Emmett immediately worried she was sick.

She reached into the car, which had every door open so Riggs could see there was no one there, and with shaking hands pulled out a canvas bag. "It's all here," she called out anxiously.

He nodded to Calvin. "Bring it here, then."

The Panthera nodded and tried to pick up the bag. She struggled but managed to half drag it across to the car. Emmett's eyes filled at the sight. He wanted to kill Riggs himself for putting her through this. As she got nearer, Emmett really started worrying because her face seemed gray and she struggled to breathe, but Riggs's grin widened the closer she got. He inhaled and nodded to himself.

Emmett's heart sank. He knew there were no wolf shifters near as Riggs would be able to smell them, and as she drew close, he could see the tightly wrapped bundles of one-hundred-dollar bills poking out of the top.

"Good girl, granny," Riggs mocked.

Regina bit her lip as it wobbled slightly, putting a shaking hand to her lips.

He glanced at Calvin and nodded to the truck. "Get in."

"No," Emmett shouted. "Calvin comes with me."

Riggs cuffed his head, and Emmett staggered, but Riggs kept a tight hold on him.

"Nah, he's already sold. Besides which, he's my insurance for getting off this mountain."

"But you promised," the Panthera said, her eyes widening and filling with moisture. "You said we could keep the pup if I agreed to come alone."

"And how do I know you haven't got a hundred cats in the trees, huh?"

"Emmett's my only grandson," Regina whispered. "I could never do anything to harm him."

Riggs scoffed. "Yeah? Then how about you do a swap? I reckon you'd make better insurance than a mutt anyway. I can offer a refund with some of this cash."

Her eyes widened. "What do you mean?"

"No," Emmett interrupted. "You can't—"

But Riggs snarled and pushed him away, reaching for the Panthera, who stumbled as he took ahold of her way too tightly. "Calvin, get here," he yelled, and Calvin scrambled back out of the truck and ran over. "Move away." Calvin looked confused but stood to the side as Riggs picked up the bag and practically dragged the Panthera to the car.

Emmett took a breath, then stilled as what looked like a dozen sleek black panthers padded out of the trees, all staring at Riggs and the Panthera. Riggs scoffed and tightened his hold. "You're out of luck, fellas. Granny's coming with me." He snarled and yanked on the Panthera. "Looks like I made the right choice."

"No," the Panthera said coolly, all trace of fragility gone. "I don't think you did." And so fast Emmett couldn't follow, she stepped to the side, ducked under Riggs's arm holding the gun, and yanked it from his hand as every cat leapt for Riggs.

Emmett looked away as Riggs's cries were cut off in a fury of snarls, fur, and blood. Footsteps came running and strong arms clasped Emmett as his hands were untied. He took a second to revel in Ryker's arms, then looked up and saw Chrissy bending down to Calvin.

"Calvin?" Calvin raised his head and met Emmett's gaze for the first time, and the hurt, recrimination, and desolation shone in his eyes before he turned away.

Emmett called out again, but Calvin huddled against Chrissy. The pain of seeing Calvin reject him was almost worse than when he had been dragged away screaming.

"Sweetheart? Are you okay?"

Marco appeared next to Ryker. "Let's sit him down."

"I can't feel him," Emmett admitted as Ryker wrapped a thermal blanket around him.

Marco quickly got out a stethoscope and pressed it to Emmett's bump. After a couple of seconds, he smiled. "He's fine. A little sleepy because of the cold, but he will wake up when we get you warmer." Emmett was led to the truck almost in a daze, and then the Panthera appeared in front of him, a tender smile on her face.

"You were amazing," Emmett whispered, knowing both he and Riggs had been had by the frail granny impersonation. With no makeup, she still looked a little older than before, but all her pretended frailty was gone. The Panthera squeezed his hand.

"Men have been underestimating me for years."

"Panthera, I can't begin—"

But she waved off Ryker's thanks. "Regina, please. Get my grandson home, and maybe we can visit after the weekend." Then she paused. "I understand you are having difficulty with the shifter council?" She smiled. "It will be dealt with."

Emmett added his thanks, and she beckoned to her panthers. One immediately shifted in time to open the car door for her. She patted his naked ass affectionately as she slid into the car.

"Did you find Michael?" Emmett asked. "Riggs told me he was building a pack. I'm worried they're holed up somewhere."

Ryker and Marco exchanged speaking glances.

"What is it?" Emmett whispered, dread coiling inside him.

"The claw found a group of caves at just about the farthest part of our territory. There was evidence there had been a lot of shifters in there, including Michael," Ryker said. "He was already dead."

"He'd definitely been killed by a predator, but we don't know what," Marco said. "To be honest, we assumed it was Riggs now that Michael had outlived his usefulness. There were at least fifteen other scent signatures. I think they'd all been living there some time, but we have no idea where they are now."

Emmett nodded and let Ryker and Marco fuss over him some more. Then he curled into Ryker's arms and closed his eyes.

CHAPTER EIGHTEEN

RYKER HAD FAILED SO SPECTACULARLY with Emmett and Calvin. Emmett was heartbroken, still not eating properly, and Calvin wouldn't go near either of them. Marco had said physically the baby was okay. Hypothermia had caused the drop in the pup's heart rate, but it had been temporary. Physically, they were both fine. Mentally was a totally different matter. He wasn't even excited to finally get the response from the shifter council naming them as pack and him as alpha. He knew Regina had kicked some wolf butts for him, and he was grateful, but it all seemed a little too late.

He rolled over and took in Emmett's pale face. "I'm moving us all into the new cabin today."

Emmett's eyes widened. "You are?"

"Being in the pack house isn't a long-term solution, but you may always have a bit of a target on you as a panther omega, and I want all three of you safe. The large bedroom with the bay window at the end will be ours and the bathroom next to it. There are three bedrooms, but Calvin can be with us for the time being, and there's room to build three more rooms on if we like."

VICTORIA SUE

Emmett shook his head. "Three more? Isn't that a little optimistic, Alpha?"

Ryker felt his face flush. "I might need an office."

Emmett smiled, then bit his lips as tears filled his eyes. Ryker gathered him into his arms.

"Hush, he's here. You're all safe." Ryker rocked him. "I've asked the Panthera to come on Saturday."

Emmett sniffed. "Thank you."

"She was incredible. We knew no other shifter could get near either of you because Riggs would scent one. We couldn't take the risk of trying to pass a panther shifter off as a human, and your dad—much as he hated to admit it—would have been no match for Riggs. He's strong but not shifter strong."

"What about whatever killed Michael?"

"Why don't you think it was Riggs?" Ryker countered.

"Because he talked about him in the present tense. He irritated him, but he wanted lackeys, followers. He said he was building a pack. There were different scent signatures. Marco said that. What if there were more omegas or even kids?"

"Calvin said he only ever saw Riggs, that after they met him, the enforcer and Michael disappeared. So, all we can do is patrol, keep an eye out and keep you safe. We're going to accept another thirty wolves this weekend, which means we can secure the compound."

"He won't even look at me," Emmett whispered, and Ryker pulled Emmett closer so he was cuddling his mate. If he lived another hundred years, he would never get sick of this.

"Give him time, sweetheart. He'll bounce back. It's just going to take time."

"I know," Emmett agreed. "He's had his whole world ripped out from under him twice."

"Do you feel well enough to get up while we move everything?"

Emmett nodded. "Yes, of course. Marco wants me to have another scan this afternoon, and I was wondering about going and seeing all the omegas."

Ryker nodded. It would help Emmett heal and get back to normal. He hoped it would help Calvin as well.

An hour later, Chrissy let herself out of the pack house and joined Ryker at the bottom of the steps. He glanced over at her. "How's Calvin?"

She shook her head. "In about the same state as Emmett, I expect. Physically, he's okay." She let the rest go unsaid, but Ryker knew.

"He doesn't trust either of us to keep him safe, and I don't know what to say to him." Because Ryker *hadn't* kept him safe. He had failed.

"If he was a human child, he'd be having therapy."

"I just called Zeke," Ryker admitted. "It's one thing he doesn't have."

"Traditionally for shifters the alpha would keep the pup with him."

Ryker frowned. "What do you mean?"

"I mean that a pup, any pup, is hardwired to go to their alpha for protection. Even if that's kicking and screaming," she added with a wry smile. "It's in his DNA. He just needs a nudge."

"A nudge?" Ryker repeated doubtfully.

"Alpha," Chrissy said with a sort of fond exasperation. "You can compel him to do as you say."

"Which might cause even more damage. He has no control, has had no control in his short life. How would being bullied, even for his own good, help?"

Chrissy was silent a moment. "You're forgetting two important things."

Ryker glanced over at her.

"He's a shifter. His biggest fear at the moment is that his security has been ripped away from him. That's similar to a human child. All children need to feel safe, but with Calvin, that doesn't mean me or even Emmett. It means you."

"But I let him down," Ryker admitted.

"You had no choice, Alpha. This time you do. You need to go show him what an alpha does. He needs to have confidence in you."

"What about Emmett?"

"That will come, but unless he feels safe, he won't be able to trust. He needs different things from Emmett."

Ryker took a deep breath and nodded. "Where is he?"

VICTORIA SUE

"Eating his breakfast, or rather pushing it around his plate," she added dryly.

Okay then. Ryker followed Chrissy back into the pack house. He'd left Emmett asleep and Fox patrolling the cabin, so he knew he had at least an hour to see if he could get anywhere. Calvin was indeed just staring at the food on his plate. Dinah was in the kitchen and kept shooting him worried glances. Chrissy deliberately hadn't come into the kitchen.

Ryker didn't go right over; he paused and thought back to all the things he'd wished for as a child growing up among shifters. The things he'd never had. The sense of belonging. The security and the family that other shifters had that he never would because his mom was a human. He never even got an official naming ceremony.

A naming ceremony.

He smiled and got out his cell phone. He called Fox and Red first and explained what he needed to happen. Then he called Zeke, and lastly, he called Regina. If anyone could get the shifter council to agree, it would be her. They were all ridiculously happy to help.

Ryker walked over to one of the bench tables and sat down opposite Calvin. He saw the little boy tense.

"I wanted to say thank you." Because apologizing wouldn't work, and Ryker had an idea that this would. Hoped anyway.

Calvin raised his head in obvious surprise, and Ryker nodded. "Because you helped to keep Emmett safe when I couldn't. He told me you gave him a drink of water. That's very important."

Calvin seemed at a loss for what to say.

"So, keeping Emmett safe is going to be your new cadet job."

Calvin looked unsure, and he still made no reply, but then he looked down at the table. "I don't want to be a gamma cadet anymore, Alpha."

"That's nonnegotiable, I'm afraid. I'm building a pack, and everyone who lives here permanently has to pitch in." Calvin still didn't reply. "Have you finished your breakfast?"

Calvin nodded, even though it didn't look like he'd eaten much of anything.

"Good, because I need you to help Fox and Red move all the things to our new rooms." He stood, and Calvin scrambled up. "Take your dishes to Dinah, please."

Calvin did, and when he came back, for the first time he looked a little curious. "You have new rooms?"

"*We* have new rooms," Ryker said and let that sink in. "Come on. Emmett can't lift anything. It might hurt the pup."

Calvin looked worried for an instant but obeyed. Knowing Calvin needed touch, even if he didn't necessarily want it, Ryker held out his hand, and after a moment, Calvin took it. Ryker would count it as a win. They met Red and Fox at the cabin. Emmett was just coming out of the bedroom as they all walked in. He smiled tentatively at Calvin, but Calvin hid behind Ryker. Ryker sent Emmett an understanding look, and Emmett sighed.

"I basically need everything emptied," Emmett said with a smile. "The new cabin has a separate bedroom for Calvin because he will be the oldest, so he gets his own room."

Calvin shot Emmett a look, but Ryker saw Emmett didn't react. Talk was cheap, as they said. This would take time.

They spent the morning moving everything, and then Emmett sat down. "My feet hurt," he gasped and sat in the big cozy armchair in the corner of their living room. Calvin, who had been pretty much ignoring Emmett, but joining in with what Ryker, Fox, and Red were doing, rushed to drag an ottoman over and planted it in front of Emmett. Emmett gulped, and everyone seemed entranced for a moment before Emmett quietly said, "Thank you."

Ryker distracted them all with food.

It was a start.

SATURDAY DAWNED BRIGHT AND EARLY. Emmett wasn't sure exactly what Ryker was up to, but whatever it was, everyone seemed to know what was happening except him. He sighed again at the busy signal he got from Kai's phone. He'd been getting it for a few days.

He felt rather than heard someone behind him and turned. To his amazement, Calvin was standing on his own, biting his lip. "Calvin, sweetheart, are you okay?"

He nodded, seeming unsure, but then held out his hand. "Alpha sent me to get you."

Emmett stood on shaky legs. He wouldn't cry. He wouldn't. He took Calvin's hand, and Calvin led him very solemnly around the back of the pack house where there were a few rows of chairs out. Ryker jogged over, thanked Calvin, and told him to go sit next to Chrissy.

"What's happening?"

"Surprise," Ryker grinned. "I thought you'd want to be here for when the Panthera and your dad get here."

"Why? I mean, of course," Emmett rushed out. "But what's going on?"

"We are officially naming the pack." Ryker looked very satisfied with himself.

"You are? That's a thing?"

Ryker grinned and led Emmett to a chair in the front row. He heard the engine of the BMW, and sure enough, in another few moments, the Panthera was escorted up to the front next to Emmett. Her claw positioned themselves around her at the edges of the clearing.

Emmett kissed her on both cheeks and marveled again at the difference in her from a few days ago. "I'm glad you're here."

Zeke walked in a moment later, and he heard the slight intake of breath from his grandmother. He walked up to them both and, smiling at Emmett, very properly turned to the Panthera and inclined his head in greeting before taking a seat next to Darriel.

Not that Emmett was surprised. His dad was here around three times a week now and spent much of that time either playing with the kids or sitting and reading Darriel's ever-increasing pile of books to him. He knew his grandmother and his dad would never truly be friends. His dad had said that, while it had obviously been Barry who had arranged for his mom's murder, he still blamed the culture surrounding the panther clans that made his mom run in the first place. Emmett was glad they could at least both be moderately pleasant to each other in the same room. He'd forgiven

BABY AND THE WOLF

his grandmother because, while he understood how his dad felt, she was doing her best to make up for it, and there was the little matter of saving his and Calvin's lives.

More people filled the seats until eventually every shifter they had was in the clearing. "I believe the Mills River pack is watching the gate," Regina whispered. "The clan of course will keep the compound safe."

Ryker stood at the front, looked at Emmett, and held out his hand.

"That's your signal," Regina stage-whispered again, and Emmett shot her a grin. She looked very pleased with herself, and he wondered why. He stood and walked up to Ryker, glad he had thought to dress prettily. His new blue shirt—according to Damien—made his eyes pop.

For a moment, he missed Kai so very much and resolved to ask Regina if she had any way of contacting him. He was sure that between her, his dad, and the Mills River pack, they might know someone.

Ryker took his hand and turned to their audience and said simply, "Welcome to the Blue Ridge pack." He waited until the cheers had died down. "I can confirm the name has been registered with the shifter council, and I would formally like to express my gratitude to the Panthera for kicking their collective shifter asses."

A smattering of laughter rose, and Emmett grinned. "Really?"

Ryker nodded, but he hadn't finished. "As of today, I officially name these shifters as members of the pack. Emmett Keefer, alpha-mate; Red Carter, head beta; Chrissy Jennings, beta; Fox Turner, beta; Marco Holt, medic." And much to Emmett's astonishment, Ryker named every single adult of the pack from memory, including all the omegas who had said they wished to join. "I also have a special and unique pack designation." Ryker tightened his fingers around Emmett's. "Zeke Coleman. Honorary beta."

Zeke's head shot up in stunned amazement, but he grinned, blushed, and accepted the cheering good-naturedly.

"Lastly," Ryker said, "we are a unique pack, and with the sanction of the council, I am announcing the new position of gamma cadet."

Emmett's hand flew to his mouth to stop a delighted cry.

"Calvin, will you please come here."

Calvin didn't seem to understand what he was being asked or was so shocked he froze for a few long seconds until Chrissy leaned down and nudged him. Then he jumped up so fast, Emmett had to blink a few times to clear his blurred vision.

Ryker held out his hand in encouragement, and Calvin rushed up to him. Ryker bent and whispered something in his ear, and Calvin nodded and stepped up next to Emmett. Emmett struggled to hold in the tears when he felt the small hand slip into his.

"Calvin, as gamma cadet I officially name you as a member of the Blue Ridge pack." There was more cheering and whistling, and Calvin leaned into Emmett for the first time since he had been snatched. "Refreshments are inside. Please help yourselves."

Ryker took Emmett's hand, and he bent and lifted Calvin up so he was at eye level. "Do you understand what I just did?"

Calvin nodded. "I'm a gamma cadet."

Ryker shot Emmett an amused smile. "Not just, buddy. I named you pack. Which means from now on, no one can ever say you have to move or live somewhere else."

Calvin's face lit up. They'd both been telling Calvin that he would never be made to leave ever again, but he clearly hadn't believed them, right up to this moment. "Really?"

Ryker nodded. "We have something else to ask you, but this is your choice. Do you understand what a choice is?"

"Sure," Calvin said promptly. "It's where I don't have to eat squash even if Dinah tells me I gotta."

Emmett gave up and wiped his eyes. "No, sweetheart," Emmett said. "This question is about who you live with. Ryker and I want you to stay with us, always. You get your own room next to ours and live with us as our son."

Then it was Calvin's turn to cry. Except Emmett knew from the excited noises he made as he threw his arms around Emmett as far as he could reach, he wasn't sad. They were finally happy tears.

CHAPTER NINETEEN

EMMETT STRETCHED his feet out in front of him and examined them carefully. Ten slightly puffy toes. He was checking because he hadn't seen them in quite a while. He blew out a breath and lay back, watching Calvin drill his gamma cadets. If Emmett had the energy, he would have chuckled, but he was exhausted and regretting reorganizing the kitchen cupboards this morning. It had started because he genuinely thought that if Ryker kept putting his favorite coffee cup in the wrong cupboard, then clearly the cups were *all* in the wrong cupboard and he needed to move them. And one cupboard led to another until he eventually needed the taller stool because he just couldn't reach.

Calvin had done well out of the deal though. Ryker had come into the kitchen and caught Emmett on the stool. The new swear jar had benefitted quite considerably in one go, and the proceeds were going toward Calvin's new bicycle. At the rate Ryker was filling it up, Calvin wasn't going to have to wait until the holidays.

He hadn't let Emmett so much as put one of his puffy toes on the floor after that. Then, he summoned Marco by bellowing as loud as he could which brought half the pack running, including Dinah who pronounced Emmett was "nesting," whatever that meant.

"Don't we have any comfier chairs?" Emmett grumbled to no one in particular. His back was killing him.

Ryker stopped his conversation with his dad and looked nonplussed. "But you loved it last week."

Emmett huffed and blew a curl out of his face. "I'm going to get my head shaved." He glanced over at his dad, hearing a chuckle, and narrowed his eyes. That had sounded suspiciously like he thought it was funny, and it wasn't at all. His dad immediately pasted an innocent expression on his face, but Emmett didn't buy it.

"Can I get you anything, love?" Ryker asked.

Emmett whined. "My back hurts. My feet hurt, and every time I even get a little bit comfy, I have to get up to pee."

Ryker hunkered down next to him. "Well, how about I take you inside and give you a foot massage?"

Zeke coughed and turned a little pink. "I'll leave you to it."

"Now you've scared my dad off," Emmett grumbled and sighed. "This is all your fault."

Ryker nodded. "Absolutely." He pulled the cover from Emmett's knees and lifted his feet off the stool, setting them down gently.

Emmett narrowed his eyes. "You don't even know what I'm blaming you for."

He grinned and leaned forward to kiss Emmett. "You're adorable when you're grumpy."

Emmett grabbed Ryker's hand and heaved himself up.

"Grumpy?" he shrieked. "I'm not grumpy." Then he paused, and before he could work out what was wrong, Ryker had swung him up into his arms. "Ryker," he whispered, his voice wobbling a little.

"Yes, my gorgeous, grumpy mate?" He beamed at him, not in the least put out about generally being blamed for everything.

"Either my water just broke, or I just peed all over you."

If a sudden pain in his back hadn't robbed Emmett of breath, Ryker's horrified face would have been funny. The bellow for Marco right in Emmett's ear wasn't, however.

"Put me down," he demanded and arched as the ache in his back developed teeth.

Ryker took absolutely no notice of him whatsoever and rushed into their cabin, carrying Emmett despite his protests. His second bellow for Marco brought most of the pack running—again. One of the new younger gammas, Samuel, was so alarmed, he shifted into his wolf, obviously expecting an alien invasion or something.

"Don't put me on the bed," Emmett shrieked again as Ryker went to lower him down. "I'm wet."

Ryker stood looking helpless until Chrissy ran in, took one look, and stripped the bed, covering it with the plastic they already had prepared, then clean sheets.

Emmett—who had previously said there was no way he was getting undressed in front of her—embraced his shifter's casualness of being naked and simply didn't care that they stripped him before putting him in a nice cool shirt they also had prepared.

Chrissy laid a small sheet over his lap and turned around while Ryker quickly washed him and made him comfortable.

Not that Emmett had any chance to appreciate it. "I thought you said this would take hours," he accused Marco as soon as he walked in. "You said I would start getting warning."

"Chrissy said you had backache." He arched an eyebrow like that was it.

"Sweetheart," Ryker soothed and took his own pants off.

"What the fuck are you doing?" Emmett gasped. "If you think you're getting out of this and going for a run—" He cut the words off and swore as the next pain took him by surprise.

Ryker smiled, going for the closet and swapping out his pants for some shorts. "They were wet. I'm going nowhere."

It was bedlam. Most of the pack seemed to think they urgently needed their alpha for something until Emmett had enough and sent everyone out except Ryker and Marco.

"Why are you so calm?" Emmett cried again in an hour when nothing seemed to be happening.

"Emmett," Marco said patiently after examining him. "You've a while to go yet. Having a baby is usually a long business. The movies always make out like women give birth in the back of a taxi, but that never happens."

"Then I want to get up," Emmett said.

"What?" Ryker spluttered before Marco had the chance.

"I want to go for a walk."

"Are you—" Ryker managed to cut off the words he probably would have regretted, but Emmett didn't care. He needed to move. They'd had about six different people in and out for the last hour, and Emmett felt like a sideshow.

"Actually, that's a good idea," Marco put in smoothly. "Helps things progress naturally."

The look Ryker sent him could have singed his beard, but Marco seemed unperturbed.

"I'm going," Emmett said determinedly. "You can come if you want."

Ryker—who had been cool, calm, and collected right up to that point—was suddenly backpedaling, but Emmett wasn't interested, and Marco just grinned and helped him on with some loose shorts.

"Shoes?"

Emmett shook his head. "No, I want to wriggle my toes in the grass."

Ryker made another suitably disgusted noise, but took Emmett's arm and supported him as he shuffled forward. He had to breathe through a contraction, but the relief on his poor back from standing up was tremendous. Marco handed Ryker a blanket, picked up one of the books Darriel had left in the room the last time he visited, and sat down in the easy chair.

Emmett yanked on Ryker's arm when he no doubt would have had an opinion on that, and they walked slowly through the big doors leading to the grassy area in front of their cabin.

"Do you want to sit in your chair?" Ryker said anxiously.

"No," Emmett said, feeling a hundred times better for being outside. Maybe it was the shifter part of him. "You keep saying pup, but what if it's a cat?"

Ryker looked at him, seeming surprised at the question. "It's a figure of speech. The likelihood of you having an omega is tremendous because of your panther line. If so, he or she may not shift at all."

Emmett stopped and caught his breath. The pain had moved under his large belly. "I think I'm ready to sit down."

Ryker spread out the blanket in the shade of the trees.

"I can't see the claw," Emmett commented after a moment of staring at the forest. "But Fox is a little obvious."

Ryker grinned sheepishly. "They just want to keep you safe, and I'm having trouble saying no to your grandmother."

Emmett nodded and blew out a breath. "Are there any pups about?" He winced as the pain started again.

"No, we made sure this area was private."

"M-hmm," Emmett said and squeezed Ryker's hand as pressure built in his belly. "Help me take the shorts off."

"Huh?" Ryker frowned.

"You said the pups weren't here," Emmett ground out as a near-constant pressure built in his abdomen.

"Emmett?" Ryker said suspiciously when Emmett started tugging at them himself.

"Now," Emmett gasped, and Ryker quickly helped him, then swore as Emmett gripped his hand really tight. He turned his head, but Emmett grabbed his arm. "I swear if you bellow for Marco one more time, you'll be sleeping alone for a year. I don't want a million people here. Omegas have been doing this for centuries." He screwed his face up, then panted as the next pain was so strong it took his breath.

"Omegas? That's *other* omegas. Not you."

Ryker in panic mode was adorable, but Emmett was stubborn. "I just want it to be us."

"Are you crazy?" Ryker yelled.

"No," Emmett gasped and rolled over. "Help me up."

"What the fuck are you doing now?" Ryker yelped as Emmett hit him in the face with his elbow, trying to move.

"What does it look like, you big oaf." Emmett gritted his teeth as Ryker helped him get up on all fours. "Sit."

VICTORIA SUE

Ryker sat obediently in front of him, and Emmett threw his arms around his neck and panted through another pain.

"Emmett," Ryker said cautiously. "I'm all for embracing nature, but there are at least five panthers, plus Fox, all looking at your bare ass now."

Emmett laughed, then moaned as a tremendous pain seemed to make his belly go rigid.

"Fuck," Ryker swore. He gave up and put his head back and shouted for Marco. He didn't bellow though, and he let Emmett burrow his head in his neck. "I had to, sweetheart," Ryker apologized. "Someone's gotta catch it."

And catch her they did. Less than seven minutes later on a blanket under the trees, Josephine Elizabeth Sullivan, after both their mom's, was born to delighted parents surrounded by four wolves and seven panthers.

Plus Fox, who had shifted back in case anyone needed an extra pair of hands. Emmett wondered sometime later if shifter births always involved naked midwives.

* * *

"ONLY YOU," Darriel murmured a few hours later when he'd had his first cuddle.

Emmett had finally consented to Ryker carrying him back to bed when Marco had finished delivering Josephine.

Darriel was showing Calvin how to properly hold his baby sister so that she was safe. Calvin was just as besotted with her as everyone else was likely to be.

Emmett sighed in contentment.

Ryker leaned back on the dresser, arms folded, a ridiculously sappy smile on his face.

"And she can be in the gamma squad, right?" Calvin asked and looked up at Ryker.

"Of course," he confirmed. "You might need her to be one of your betas one day when you're alpha."

Calvin seemed to consider that carefully, then nodded his approval.

BABY AND THE WOLF

Ryker stepped over. "Why don't you give her to me, then you can go and see if Dinah's cookies have come out of the oven?"

Calvin bent down and kissed his sister's head, then let Ryker take her. He scrambled off the bed and headed to the door.

"Hey!" Emmett prompted indignantly.

Calvin grinned and rushed back, climbed none too gently onto the bed and smacked a kiss on Emmett's cheek before giggling, jumping down, and running out of the door.

Darriel also excused himself. They'd had a ton of visitors. His dad had just left, and Emmett was ready for a long-ass nap.

"Happy, omega-mine?" Ryker laid a sleeping baby in the very expensive crib her delighted great-grandma had bought her, took Emmett's hand and kissed his palm.

"Very," Emmett whispered and tilted his chin for a kiss. Ryker was quick to oblige, then eased himself very gently onto the bed and took Emmett into his arms.

"I love you," Ryker murmured after a moment. "All three of you," he added fondly.

* * *

EMMETT'S CELL phone rang sometime later after he had fed Josie. She was back asleep, cuddled in Ryker's arms. He'd already spoken to Regina, but he answered it anyway, shooting Ryker a rueful smile.

"Emmett?"

Emmett froze. "Kai?" He sounded awful. "What is it?" He heard quiet sobs, then some shouting, and Kai gasped.

"Please, you gotta come and get me. My alpha's dead, and they've taken Maddox." He gasped. "They're selling us and—" The words were cut off with a cry.

With shaky fingers, Emmett tried to call back, but it rang once, then went to voicemail. He tried a second time, and it said that person was not accepting calls.

Ryker bent and gave him Josie, taking the phone and calling Red.

Emmett listened in horror as Ryker repeated what they had both heard. Ryker instructed Red to call their contacts and see what they could find out. He finally put Emmett's phone back on the nightstand and sat on the bed.

Tears were running down Emmett's face. "He said they were selling him."

Ryker nodded grimly. "I heard." He bent down and brushed a kiss on Josie's forehead, then Emmett's lips. "We'll find him."

Emmett gazed at the man he adored. He knew Ryker would do anything he could for him; he just wasn't sure if rescuing Kai and his baby could be one of them.

Don't miss out on the free prequel, *Baby and the Bear*, available as a free download at Bookfunnel or Prolific Works.

Love MPreg?
Check out these series and single title by Victoria Sue.

Sirius Wolves Series
According to legend, when humankind is at its most desperate, the goddess Sirius will send three of the most powerful werewolf shifters ever created to save mankind. The alphas, Blaze, Conner and Darric, find their omega in Aden. They become true mates, fulfilling the ancient prophecy and forming Orion's Circle. Now, the battle against terrorist group The Winter Circle has begun.

Daddy's Girl
An Alpha who hates omegas. An omega who hates Alphas. Forced together by circumstances, both men are determined to see their arrangement through.

Except the longer they stay together, neither of them is sure they want it to end.

His First Series
Omegaverse at it's finest! Set in the future, these novels pack in all the feels, while still wrapping up with a wonderfully sweet ending. Whether you've never tried MPREG or you're just looking for your next favorite Alpha/Omega pairing, check out the His First series.

Hunter's Creek Series
The Hunter's Creek novels will draw you in with action and keep you hooked until each satisfying HEA. This series won't disappoint fans of shifters, fated mates or MPREG.

Kingdom of Askara Series
The Kingdom of Askara has been torn apart by conflict for centuries, where humans exist as subservient beings to their werewolf masters. Legend says it will only be able to heal itself when an Alpha King and a pure omega are mated and crowned together, but a pure omega hasn't been born in over a thousand years.

FREE PREQUEL

Baby and the Bear

For a cuddly middle-aged accountant Seth was having a bad day. His boyfriend had dumped him. He'd narrowly avoided hitting a wild bear and crashed his car. He was lost in a snow storm, and likely to die of hypothermia. The only shelter he could find seemed to have been already claimed by the wild bear that he'd nearly hit earlier, and now looked at him like he'd make a nice snack.

Bear shifter Jesse's whole year had started bad and gone downhill from there. He was in labor and if his family found him they would kill his cub. He needed help. He needed a miracle.

When the human he'd tried to frighten away not only refused to go and became his surrogate midwife, Jesse began to wonder if he'd finally found one.

Don't miss out on the prequel, *Baby and the Bear*, available as a free download at Bookfunnel or Prolific Works.

ABOUT VICTORIA SUE

Victoria Sue fell in love with love stories as a child when she would hide away with her mom's library books and dream of the dashing hero coming to rescue her from math homework. She never mastered math but never stopped loving her heroes and decided to give them the happy ever afters they fight so hard for.

She loves reading and writing about gorgeous boys loving each other the best—and creating a family for them to adore. Thrilled to hear from her readers, she can be found most days lurking on Facebook where she doesn't need factor 1000 sun-cream to hide her freckles.

www.victoriasue.com

For the latest news, deals, stories and more, sign up for Victoria Sue's Newsletter.

Join Victoria Sue's Crew (Facebook reader group) to discuss all things Victoria Sue, to participate in member only contests, and more!

facebook.com/victoriasueauthor

twitter.com/vickysuewrites

instagram.com/victoriasueauthor

bookbub.com/authors/victoria-sue

amazon.com/author/victoriasue

ALSO BY VICTORIA SUE

Standalone Novels

Daddy's Girl*

An Alpha who hates omegas. An omega who hates Alphas. Forced together by circumstances, both men are determined to see their arrangement through. Except the longer they stay together, neither of them is sure they want it to end.

Series

Unexpected Daddies

Daddy kink with heart and heat. No ABDL.

Heroes and Babies

Protective men find love while fighting to save a child. Contemporary suspense with heart-pounding action.

Guardians of Camelot

Hundreds of years ago, facing defeat, the witch Morgana sent monsters into the future to vanquish a humanity King Arthur wouldn't be able to save. The King might have won the battle, but now, centuries later, a few chosen men will have to fight the war. To battle an ancient evil, the greatest weapon each hero will have is each other.

Enhanced World

This series follows an enhanced H.E.R.O. team to provide the right mix of action and romance. This series is the perfect for fans of romance with a blend of military/law enforcement, urban fantasy and superheroes. As one reviewer put it, "This story was like S.W.A.T. meets X-men meets The Fantastic Four."

His First*

Omegaverse at it's finest! Set in the future, these novels pack in all the feels, while still wrapping up with a wonderfully sweet ending. Whether you've never tried MPREG or you're just looking for your next favorite Alpha/Omega pairing, check out the His First series.

Rainbow Key

Rainbow Key is an idyllic island retreat off the west coast of Florida. Think wedding destination, white sandy beaches, lurve... except at the moment Joshua is struggling to pay the electricity bill, they've no paying customers, and even if they did they can't afford the repairs from the devastating hurricane that struck three years ago. Then there's Matt who just got let out of prison, Charlie who ran away from home, and Ben, a famous model until a devastating house fire destroyed his face. Welcome to Rainbow Key — held together by love, family, and sticky tape.

Kingdom of Askara*

The Kingdom of Askara has been torn apart by conflict for centuries, where humans exist as subservient beings to their werewolf masters. Legend says it will only be able to heal itself when an Alpha King and a pure omega are mated and crowned together, but a pure omega hasn't been born in over a thousand years.

Sirius Wolves*

According to legend, when humankind is at its most desperate, the goddess Sirius will send three of the most powerful werewolf shifters ever created to save mankind. The alphas, Blaze, Conner and Darric, find their omega in Aden. They become true mates, fulfilling the ancient prophecy and forming Orion's Circle. Now, the battle against terrorist group The Winter Circle has begun.

Innocents

A captivating historical duology set in Regency London. **The Innocent Auction:** *It started with a plea for help and ended with forbidden love, the love between a Viscount and a stable-boy. An impossible love and a guarantee of the hangman's noose.* **The Innocent Betrayal:** *Two broken souls. One so damaged he thinks he doesn't deserve love, and one so convinced he would never find it he has stopped looking. Danger, lies, and espionage. The fate of hundreds of English soldier's lives depending on them to trust each other, to work together.*

Pure

A madman has been kidnapping, torturing and murdering submissives. Join Callum, Joe and Damon as they race against the clock to stop the killings, while they each find love with a submissive. This trilogy of romantic thrillers is set against the backdrop of BDSM club Pure.

Hunter's Creek*

The Hunter's Creek novels will draw you in with action and keep you hooked until each satisfying HEA. This series won't disappoint fans of shifters, fated mates or MPREG.

*Stories may contain MPREG

Printed in Great Britain
by Amazon